Henry Seton Merriman

Prisoners and Captives

Vol. III

Henry Seton Merriman

Prisoners and Captives
Vol. III

ISBN/EAN: 9783744755900

Printed in Europe, USA, Canada, Australia, Japan

Cover: Foto ©Andreas Hilbeck / pixelio.de

More available books at **www.hansebooks.com**

PRISONERS AND CAPTIVES

BY

HENRY SETON MERRIMAN

AUTHOR OF

"YOUNG MISTLEY," "THE PHANTOM FUTURE," "SUSPENSE"

IN THREE VOLUMES

VOL. III.

LONDON

RICHARD BENTLEY AND SON

Publishers in Ordinary to Her Majesty the Queen

1891

CONTENTS OF VOLUME III.

PRISONERS AND CAPTIVES.

CHAPTER I

FROM AFAR.

ONE morning, about a fortnight later, Matthew Mark Easton received a letter which caused him to leave his breakfast untasted and drive off in the first hansom-cab he could find to Tyars' club.

The waiter whose duty it was to look after the few resident members, informed the American, whom he knew well by sight, that Mr. Tyars was not down-stairs yet.

"Well," replied Easton, "I guess I'll

wait for him; in fact I am going to have breakfast with him—a boiled egg and two pieces of thin toast."

He was shown into the room occupied by Tyars, and proceeded to make himself exceedingly comfortable, in a large arm-chair, with the morning newspaper.

Tyars was not long in making his appearance—trim, upright, strong as usual, and conveying that unassertive sense of readiness for all emergencies which was at times almost aggressive. He carried his hand in the smallest and most unobtrusive sling allowed by the faculty. At his heels walked Muggins—the grave, the pink-eyed. Muggins was far too gentlemanly a dog to betray by sign or sound that he considered this visitor's behaviour a trifle too familiar.

" Good morning—captain," said Easton, cheerily. " Well, Muggins—I trust I see you in the enjoyment of health."

The violent chuck under the chin with which this hope was emphasized, received scant acknowledgment from a very stumpy tail. The truth was that Matthew Mark Easton was no great favourite with Muggins. He was not his sort. Muggins had never been a frivolous dog, and now that puppyhood was past, he affected a solemnity of demeanour worthy of his position in life. He looked upon the American as a man lacking self-respect.

"I have news," said Easton at once, laying aside the newspaper; "news from old Smith—Pavloski Smith."

"Where from?" inquired Tyars, without enthusiasm.

"From Tomsk! It is most extraordinary how these fellows manage to elude the police. Here is old Pavloski—an escaped Siberian exile—a man they would give their boots to lay their hands on—goes back to

Russia, smuggles himself across the German frontier, shows that solemn face of his unblushingly in Petersburg, and finally posts off to Tomsk with a lot of contraband luggage as a merchant. I thought I had a fair allowance of check, but these political fellows are far ahead of me. Their check and their calm assurance are simply unbounded!"

"The worst of it," said Tyars, turning over his letters with small interest, "is that the end is always the same. They all overdo it sooner or later."

"Yes," admitted the American, whose sensitive face betrayed a passing discomfort; "but it is no good thinking of that now."

"Not a bit," acquiesced Tyars, cheerfully. "Only I shall be rather surprised if I meet those three men up there. It would be better luck than one could reasonably expect."

"If one of them gets through with his party, all concerned should be very well pleased with themselves," said Easton. "Now listen to what Pavloski says."

He unfolded a letter, which was apparently a commercial communication written on the ordinary mail paper of a merchant, and bearing the printed address of an office in Cronstadt.

On the first page was a terse advice, written in a delicate clerkly hand, of the receipt by Hull steamer of a certain number of casks containing American apples.

"This," said Easton, "is from our stout friend. He has received the block soups, and the Winchester cartridges."

He then opened the letter farther, and on the two inside pages displayed a closely written communication in a peculiar pink-tinted ink, which had evidently been brought to light by some process, for the paper was wrinkled and blistered.

"'I have,'" read the American, slowly, as if deciphering with difficulty, "'reached Tomsk without mishap, travelling with an ordinary civilian post-pass, which is very little slower at this time of year, as there are plenty of horses. I have bought a strong sledge, wholly covered in—the usual sledge of a merchant of fine goods—and instead of sleeping in the stations, usually lie down on the top of my cases under the cover. I give as reason for this the information that I have many valuables—watches, rings, trinkets—and being a young merchant, cannot run the risk of theft to save my own personal comfort. I have travelled day and night, according to the supply of horses, but have always succeeded hitherto in communicating with those who are to follow me. One man on my list was not in the

prison indicated—he is probably dead. I
find great improvements. Our organization
is more mechanical, and not so hysterical—
this I attribute to the diminished number of
female workers. All the articles with which
your foresight provided me have been useful; but the great motor in Siberia is
money. With the funds I have at my
disposal I feel as powerful as the Czar.
I can buy whom I like, and what I like.
My only regret is that the name of C. T.
has to be suppressed—that the hundreds
of individuals who will benefit by his grand
generosity will never know the name of the
Englishman who has held out his laden
hands to those groaning under the yoke of
a barbarous oppression. When we are all
dead—when Russia is free, his name will
be remembered by some one. The watches
will be very useful; I have sold two at a
high price; but once beyond Irkutsk, and I

will sell or give one to the master of each important station, or to the starosti of each village. By this means those who follow me will know that they are on the right track. They cannot well stop at a station, or halt in a village, without being shown the watch, which will tell them that one of us is in front. I have enough watches to lay a train from Irkutsk to the spot where I assemble my party. I met my two companions by appointment at the base of the Ivan Veliki tower in the Kremlin, and we spent half an hour in the cathedral together within a musket-shot of the Czar, and under the very nose of the cream of his police. Since then we have not met, but are each working forward by the prescribed route alone. I see great changes here—Russia is awakening—she is rubbing her eyes. God keep you all three!'"

Matthew Mark Easton indicated by a little

jerk of the head that the letter was finished. Then after looking at it curiously for a moment, he folded it and put it away in his pocket.

"Old Smith," he said, "waxes quite poetic at times."

"Yes," answered Tyars, pouring out his coffee, "but there is a keen business man behind the poetry."

"One," observed Easton in his terse way, "of the sharpest needles in Russia, and quite the sharpest in Siberia at the present moment."

"He will need to be; though I think that the worst of his journey is over. The cream is, as he says, at Moscow. Once beyond Nijni he will find milk, then milk-and-water, and finally beyond Irkutsk the thinnest water. The official intellect in Siberia is not of a brilliant description. Pavloski can outwit every gendarme or

Cossack commandant he meets, and once out of Irkutsk they need not fear the law. They will only have Nature to compete with, and Nature always gives fair play. When they have assembled they will retreat north like an organized army before a rabble, for there are not enough Cossacks and gendarmes in Northern Siberia to form anything like an efficient corps of pursuit. They may follow, but I shall have the fugitives on board and away long before they reach the seaboard."

"How many are there in Yakutsk?"

"Two thousand altogether, soldiers and Cossacks. They have no means of transport and no commissariat corps. By the time that the news travels south to Yakutsk, that there is a body of supposed exiles to the north, our men will have gained such an advantage that pursuit would be absurd."

"It seems," replied Easton, "so very

simple, that I wonder no one has tried it before."

. At this moment the waiter entered the room with several hot dishes, but the two men went on discussing openly the question mooted. Club-waiters are the nearest approach to a human machine that modern civilization has yet produced.

" Simply because no one has had the money. I know several whaling captains who would be ready enough to try, provided they were paid ! The worst danger was the chance of the three men being captured as soon as they entered Russia. They are now at their posts in Siberia. In May they meet surreptitiously on the southern slope of the Verkoianiska, cross the mountains, and they are safe. The three leaders will then be together, and they will retreat north as arranged, scaring the Yamschicks into obedience, and taking

all the post-deer and dogs with them, so
that an immediate pursuit will be impossible.   I think," added the organizer of this
extraordinary plot, " that we shall succeed."

Easton was silent. His boiled egg had
arrived, and his keen little face was screwed
up into earnest inquiry as he gently broke
the shell with a spoon. He was a strange
mixture of the trivial and the great, this
sharp-witted American ; but he was intensely conscious of his own shallowness.
He could touch great things, but he could
not grasp them ; he could give attention to
trifles, but he could not allot to them just
that modicum of thought which would
suffice.   In the position which he had occupied during the last two months, namely,
the chief superintendent of trifles, he was
excellent.   But without the directing control of Claud Tyars he would probably have
given all his attention to small things, neg-

lecting or fearing to touch the great. He would have regarded the pence too closely, failing to make sure that the pounds were safe. There was no lack of courage, but a distinct want of power, and this deficiency became singularly apparent in intercourse with Claud Tyars.

We very often meet men in the world who have done one thing; conceived some great thought, or invented one great combination—say a soda-water cork. Upon that one basis they seem to rest for the remainder of their days. He does not manufacture the soda-water cork, he does not even attend to the advertisement of it ; but he invented it long years back in the recesses of a youth which can hardly have been brilliant. One is conscious that he is a great man, or that he should be such, and yet there is a wondering desire to know why he does not get up and invent something else—a machine to cut and read magazines, or something equally in demand.

This was to some extent the position of Matthew Mark Easton at the beginning of the year which has been succeeded by four. He had conceived the idea which Claud Tyars and his intrepid colleagues had now quite wrested from his grasp. The initial conception had so grown and expanded, had gathered in here and shot out there, in such a manner as to render it quite strange in the eyes of its own father.

It was not a pleasant position, but the American faced it pluckily. He was to some extent an imaginative little man—had been an imaginative boy. He had dreamed dreams just as some others have dreamed them. He had nourished 'and fostered great ambitions—just as you, my good friend, may have done—just as a poor scribbler *may* have done. We confess nothing, mind you !

but there may have been a time . . . And
now Easton had met a man, made a friend
of a man, who calmly showed him that those
same dreams were woefully hollow. It is a
strange fatuity, that habit of dreaming. At
the very threshold of life we ought by rights
to recognize what lies before us. At the
very earliest school we attend we probably
find that a large portion of our companions
are infinitely cleverer than ourselves; in
the playground, on football or cricket field,
we are bound to realize that there are better
players than ourselves. And so on, as we
reach out into the world. We find better
shots, better dancers, better oars, better
seats in the saddle; and perhaps better
thinkers, better writers, better workers,
better wooers. But—does all this shake
that strange, deep-rooted confidence in self?
Does it open our eyes to the melancholy
fact that we are not only like other people,

but inferior to them. Does it, I ask in all gravity, make you and me acknowledge that this life that we are leading now is, humanly speaking, permanent; that it is the only life we shall ever have, and that it is after all rather a sorry business? No. We go on in a futile way, building up grand dreams beneath our gray hairs, vainly looking to that day when we shall be blest, when we shall be celebrated, and recognized as the great men that we are. And yet at times there comes a fleeting glimpse of the reality. Some one passes us in the race, or does something that we should like to have done, and for a moment our hearts are pressed down with the uncomfortable feeling of being left behind.

This was precisely the feeling which had stolen into the cheery heart of Matthew Mark Easton while he opened his egg with that singular attention which has been pre-

viously indicated. When I am a ghost,
endowed with the power of looking into
men's minds, I shall not peer through the
grave eyes, but through the smiling. I shall
not flit about among those who weep, but
among such as will not weep because they
are too courageous.

"Of course, old man," said Easton, "you
—*we* shall succeed. Pass the salt, please."

Nothing escaped his keen observation.
He knew well enough that he could not play
a greater part, and yet there had been placed
in his frail frame that longing for action felt
at one time or other by all men worth their
salt. He did not glance enviously at his
friend's huge limbs and quick strength of
carriage, for he was accustomed to it. He
was accustomed to his own incapacity.

It is probable that Claud Tyars knew
something of his friend's feelings upon this
subject, for he never made reference to his

own share of the exploit beyond what was
absolutely necessary. Whatever he may
have felt, he never exulted openly in the
coming dangers by sea and ice. Their conversation was chiefly respecting the progress
of the three adventurous Russians headed
by Sergius Pavloski, and the probabilities of
their failure or success. It was a safe subject;
for neither Claud Tyars nor Matthew Mark
Easton could have attempted what these
men were undertaking.

CHAPTER II.

AN OVERTURE.

THERE are some—indeed many—people who shun the world because they fear it. Not being sure of its admiration they prefer to avoid the risk of earning its contempt. But there are others who withdraw themselves because there exists in their hearts an honest and unobtrusive contempt for the opinion of that generality which is usually called " the world." Of these latter was Claud Tyars, and it must be allowed that his opinion was in no way aggressive or offensive. He despised the generality of his fellow-men, but he was quite unconscious of so doing. He had lived his short life among men of a race singularly unaffected by the blame or praise of the world—the British upper middle-class. In most moral virtues or faults it is merely a question of degree, and it is therefore comprehensible that Claud Tyars should be unaware of the fact that he carried the peculiarity of his contemporaries to an excess.

It was now a well-known topic of the day that he was fitting up an Arctic expedition, and the society papers had taken good care to make the most of the terrible defence of the stage-box in the Epic Theatre on the historical night of the panic. The majority of his friends knew that his arm had been broken in that struggle for life, and his refusal of all invitations was therefore a matter of small surprise.

It seemed hardly natural for a man of

his character to fear a little unsought publicity, but this excuse he invariably put forward when rallied by his friends for unsociability.

Easton knew no more than the rest of the world why Tyars so suddenly withdrew himself from all social intercourse. They had moved in the same circles to a somewhat limited extent, and had never been coupled as men likely to be found together. It was only by degrees, therefore, that he learnt of Tyars' defection from the duties of a man placed in the midst of the most thoroughly sociable community in the world. From Miss Winter, Easton learnt that Tyars had never even called upon her or at Brook Street, to inquire whether any after effects had shown themselves since the memorable evening of the fire.

The relationship between the two men was just one of those understandings which

are impossible between women, and common
enough among their husbands, brothers, and
sons.   A friendship between women is
usually comprehensive—it embraces the
lives of both from morning till night without
reservation.   They are friends indoors, in
their bed-rooms ; at luncheon, at dinner,
at dances, and between those functions.
If they meet at night they are straightway
consumed with a desire to meet in the
morning.   They want to shop together, to
lunch together, and to take each other up-
stairs to see their new hats.   If they are
unmarried they talk about young men
and the millinery means of fascinating the
same ; if they are married they discuss the
weaknesses, physical or mental, of their
husbands, and the best treatment for same.
They do not even stop there, but go on to
compare cooks, and even exchange a receipt
or two.

Now with men it is different. We have out-door friends and in-door friends. Old March Brown, for instance, is a first-rate fellow, an excellent sportsman, the keenest fisherman that ever wet a wader; but in a ball-room he is no friend of mine—I hate him! We have fished together in Norway and Greenland, but I do not even know his wife's name, nor his cook's besetting sin.

Then there is young Adonis Smiler. He is usually the best dancer in the room; it is a pleasure to take him out as one's friend. He always gives satisfaction to his hostess, and several freshly-bloomed young ladies invariably think of him the next morning. But because we take each other out to dances, Smiler does not, any more than I, propose spending our autumn holiday together. No; Smiler is a London friend, and nothing else —he is an evening friend. By daylight he is an effeminate dandy, and I should not

think of being on the same moor as Smiler
were he in the possession of a gun.

A friend of mine came in to see me a
few minutes ago, interrupting the flow of
these remarkable observations. For five
years he has been diametrically under my
feet; we have always kept half a world
between us, and we have never thought of
corresponding. He is an antipodean friend,
and we have become quite accustomed to
thinking of each other as in the antipodes.
In fact, each formed part of the other's
antipodes. We took up the same questions
that we left unsettled five years ago, and
so far as I could gather, the friendship
has in no way cooled, though we have
never met twice in the same part of the
world.

In a word, the friendship of women means
the possession of many, if not all, interests
in common; while men can build up the

enduring fabric upon the basis of one mutual interest only.

Matthew Mark Easton possessed mental energy of a conceptive order ; Claud Tyars was a healthy Hercules, his body longed for work. They were brought together by that vague influence we call Chance, and they found a common interest at once. But their friendship, which lasted as long as human friendships can last, was never general. They never knew much of each other's lives. The great absorbing interest of their existence during these years had never flagged ; there had always been some point or another requiring instant discussion, and they never found time to talk of themselves or of each other.

The Americans are the most independent people of the world. They have learnt more thoroughly than any other race the great lesson that whatever may be done for

us in the hereafter we must look after
ourselves now. They expect no help and
they ask none. Easton was a true American
in his social proclivities; he was not the
man to overstep those tacit boundaries
by which men's friendships are confined.
So long as things went on satisfactorily, so
long as Tyars attended to the outfit of ship
and crew, he was free to live where he liked
and how he liked.

Oswin Grace was naturally brought into
daily communication with Tyars, but they
met at the docks, usually on board their
vessel, and at evening they parted without
question of meeting later. The young officer,
accustomed as he was to obedience, had by
this time quite fallen under the influence
of his chief, and their relationship towards
each other was therefore slightly altered.

Miss Winter, however, was a woman of
resource. For reasons of her own she de-

termined to bring Claud Tyars out of his
shell. It was nothing to her that the
exploring vessel should be out of dry-dock
and almost ready for sea, her crew engaged,
her stores on board. She had one card
left, and she played it with that calm
assurance which follows on skilful courage.
And so it came about that Muggins set up
a great barking, and displayed a determination to repel or die, one morning when
breakfast had been cleared away by the
lightning-fingered club-waiter.

The diminutive buttons attached to the
hall-door knocked, entered, and stood aside
in three movements, like the soldier's son
that he was.

"Admiral Grace—sir," he announced,
clippingly.

Then Muggins, obeying one terse word,
retired under the arm-chair nearest to the
fire.

The admiral entered with some dignity and laid his stick and hat upon the table; then he turned round and glared at the button-boy, causing the door to be shut precipitately.

"Good morning, sir!" said Tyars, pleasantly. He was standing, but did not offer his hand. He had a singular and almost foreign way of avoiding the practice of shaking hands, and now that his right arm was disabled he never offered his left.

The admiral looked at him, and then held out his hand very deliberately, so that no mistake could be made.

"Good morning," he said; "your hand."

He took the reluctant fingers held out, it must be confessed, rather awkwardly, in a good hearty, old-fashioned grip.

"I came," said the old gentleman so concisely that Tyars almost wondered whether he had asked aloud the question that was in his mind, "to your club because I have something to say to you."

He stopped, visibly embarrassed, in a bluff, undisguised manner; his kindly but firm lips moved as if framing tentative words.

"It is," Tyars hastened to say, "a beastly morning. I hope you have not got wet."

"Thanks, no; I am not afraid of a little clean water." He pulled himself up and looked somewhat pugnacious. "I came about a matter which—I have something to say which is not easy for an old fellow to say to a young one."

"Oh!" Tyars drew forward a chair in a pleasant and comfortable way—it was, by the way, a remarkably comfortable chair. "Won't you sit down? Put your boots on the fender, your right foot is wet, these roads are so badly kept."

"D—n it, sir," said the admiral, without accepting the chair, "I didn't come here to talk about my boots."

Tyars looked at him in his large placid way—as one sees a huge Newfoundland look at a fox-terrier. He made no further attempt to stave it off, for he knew that it had come. He was a man who hated thanks and apologies, and never learnt to receive them graciously.

And so they stood opposite to each other—two typical Englishmen—an old and a young sailor. Not poetical, nor romantic, nor highly intellectual—you are not asked to imagine that. But—honest! Honest and strong. Surely the Creator meant men to be both these; for if they are, no woman need fear to love them.

"I came," said the old mariner, fixing his solemn gray eyes upon his companion's face, "to ask you to accept an apology.

If I do it badly it is because I have had no practice at that sort of thing."

" Please," interrupted Tyars, gravely, " do not say anything more. There must be some mistake. I know of nothing that could require an apology, and I am like yourself—I know nothing of such matters. Won't you sit down ?"

This time the admiral accepted. He sat squarely down, undeterred ; he was fully bent upon hammering out what he considered his dutiful apology.

" It is," he said, in a more conversational manner, " like this. When you first came home, and Oswin brought you in to dinner, I took a dislike to you. I—well, I thought you were a humbug—what the Frenchmen call a *poseur.* Perhaps I was a bit jealous about that merchantman you brought home —I would rather have had my boy commanding her, and you playing second fiddle.

Then there is another thing. I am afraid I am a little jealous of all young fellows who come to my house and cut an old fogey out; you understand? My girl—my little girl, Helen."

" Yes," answered Tyars, slowly, " I understand."

" I think a lot of her," said the old fellow, with an apologetic laugh, " and I am always imagining that every man who sees her is going to fall in love with her. Ha! ha!"

" Ha! ha!" echoed Tyars, with sudden gaiety.

" Stupid of me," added the admiral, " but I can't help it, you know!"

" Ha! ha!" repeated Claud Tyars, in identical tones.

" Well," continued Admiral Grace, settling himself more comfortably in the large chair, " it all comes to this. I have found out my mistake all round, and I wanted to

tell you that I consider you are a gentleman and a sailor, and I am proud to know
you."

He pulled out his cuffs, and emitted a
long breath of relief. Like a great school-
boy, he had gravely made up his mind to
say this thing, and now that it was over
he was fairly well pleased with the manner
in which he had managed to say it.

"It is very good of you to say so," replied
Tyars, rather lamely, for he was a poor hand
at turning glib phrases. "By your own
showing, however, no apology was necessary.
It was only a matter of thoughts, and we
are all free to think what we like."

"Then," said the old gentleman with a
chuckle, "I did not show my dislike?"

"Not that I noticed," replied Tyars. He
wisely refrained from adding that this might
be because he had never taken the trouble
to look.

"That's all right. And now, my boy, I want to thank you for your bravery and coolness the other night. From what I hear, you undoubtedly saved my little girl's life—if not the lives of the whole party. It quite turned the tables on me. It was quite contrary to what I was thinking of you, you see. That broken arm too—I hope you did it saving Helen."

"I did," answered the young fellow, with a quick, unnatural laugh; "but why do you hope that?"

"Because," replied Admiral Grace, gravely, "it must be much more satisfactory to an English sailor to think that he carried away a spar in saving another life than his own—the life of a woman and a pretty girl too. Helen wants to thank you herself, which she somehow forgot to do. Will you come and dine one night, and give her a chance? Name your own night."

Claud Tyars did not seem to hesitate. He bowed gravely, while his beard and moustache moved as if he were biting his lip in order to control some passing emotion.

"Thank you," he said, "very much ; but I am afraid I must refuse. I am so busy that I have entirely given up going out."

"As you like," snapped the admiral, after a little pause. He was vexed, and did not care to disguise it. He naturally concluded that Tyars bore him ill-feeling despite the apology which had been so difficult for him to make. It was no hard matter to divine this from the proud old man's sudden hauteur of manner ; and Claud Tyars doubtless saw it, for his unobtrusive gaze had never left his companion's face. It was rather strange that he did not hasten to undeceive his visitor, to protest that nothing could have given him greater pleasure than to dine at Brook Street. He might easily have put forward another excuse. It was a matter requiring very little to smooth it, but the young Englishman deliberately left it as it was—left his refusal in all its curt formality for the old martinet to put in his pipe and smoke at leisure.

He stood where he had stood during the entire interview, with his one able hand resting on the back of a chair. His attitude and expression were distinctly courteous, and—nothing more. It is, one finds, these grave men who are so difficult to read. One may hide many things, many sorrows and loves and hatreds behind a ready smile; but a pleasant, dense gravity is much more impenetrable.

Admiral Grace rose, gave one quick glance at his companion's face, and then took up his hat and stick.

"I am due at the Admiralty," he said. "Good morning."

Tyars followed him towards the door, gravely respectful. He opened the door and followed him down the thickly-carpeted stairs. Half-way the old man stopped.

"By the way," he said, raising his stick, "Miss Winter asked me to deliver a message. She has found a berth for a *protégé* of yours, the son of your carpenter. She will be in at eleven o'clock to-morrow morning if you can find time to call and see her about it."

"Thank you. I will try to do so."

"Good morning."

"Good morning."

And the old fellow stumped out into the sunny street. A woman would have taken his last words as a confession that he had been sent by Miss Winter—some men might have read it so, but Claud Tyars was not of these.

CHAPTER III.

TRAPPED.

THE next morning he despatched his laborious correspondence as quickly as a cramped left hand would allow. He was not dressed in the tar-stained old suit donned for dock-work, but in blue serge.

Armed with a cigar to keep out the morning coolness, he set off westward at a swinging pace, and deliberately walked into the trap set for him by Miss Winter. This was so simple, and it succeeded so smoothly, that the lady whose well-intentioned deceit it was stood almost breathless in her own bedroom, pressing her hand to her breast and wondering whether she should laugh or cry.

The maid answering his summons swung the door so wide open as to leave no doubt of his welcome and expectation. Miss Winter was in, would he step up-stairs? This he did with rather less agility than when he had possessed two arms to swing. He was shown into the drawing-room, and for a moment imagined himself alone. Then he was conscious of a sound of smooth dress material, and a young lady rose from the music-stool, partially concealed by the piano placed cornerwise near the window. It was a gloomy morning, and the lady stood with her back towards the light, and her face consequently in the shadow. But Tyars saw at once that this was not Agnes Winter; indeed the sight (as pleasant a one as any man could wish to look upon) brought a quick contraction of pain to eyes

and lips. He knew only too well every
sweet curve and outline of head and form
placed in graceful silhouette against the
lace curtains.

They knew that they had been both
tricked, and the sudden knowledge of it
seemed to sweep all social formula away, for
they never greeted each other. Something
in the girl's attitude (for he could not see
her glowing eyes) told the man then that
he had not this thing to bear alone.
His sorrow was hers; that which weighed
upon his broad back almost crushed her
slight young shoulders beneath its weight.
This great heavenly light, this opaque
darkness, had crept into her heart as into
his, against the defence of a stubborn will.
It was so new to both, so utterly surprising,
so completely unlooked for, that both alike
were dazed. Since its advent, both had
walked on with uncertain steps, staggering

vaguely beneath a new and wholly bewildering responsibility; something that seemed to have no beginning and no end on earth; something that tugged at the heart and cast a great veil of indifference over all pleasures and all trivial occupations; something that brings our every-day life suddenly forward like a cunning stage-light cast from the wings, and builds up behind the daily round of toil and pleasure a vague shimmering perspective of which you dimmest distance is Heaven — and nothing else.

When a strong man gets a fever, the doctor shakes his head: when a strong heart has this pain it is pain indeed.

At last the girl moved. She came towards him, only a few paces, and then stopped. She had emerged from the shadow, and the whiteness of her face struck him like a blow.

"Agnes," she said, steadily, "has just gone up-stairs."

He nodded his head in a sharp, comprehensive way which had been acquired at sea.

"I did not expect to find you here," was his reply, less inconsequent than might at first appear.

She crossed the room, passing close by him, so that a breath of cool air reached him, and went towards the mantel-piece. Her intention was evidently to ring the bell, but her strength of purpose seemed to fail her at the last moment, and she stood undecided upon the white fur hearth-rug with her back turned towards him.

"Had you known— ?" she began.

"I think," he completed, "that I should not have come."

Her eyelids quivered for a second, and the faintest suggestion of a very sad smile

flickered across her lips. He did not know
that he was making matters worse, making
her burden doubly heavy. He did not
know that this very strength of his was
what she loved. He was very far from
suspecting that she had foreseen his answer
before she asked the strange question. He
would have been intensely surprised to
learn that, although her back was turned
towards him, she saw his attitude, the
quiescent strength of each limb (denoting
subtly the inner strength of the soul) as
he stood upright, patient, and gentle, tearing out his iron heart and trampling it
underfoot. He never saw the shadowy
little smile, nor knew its pathetic meaning.

And so he kept his secret, he held his
peace despite a gnawing temptation to
speak. He allowed her to continue thinking, if so indeed she thought, that he was
sacrificing her to his own ambition, as

Miss Winter honestly believed. He never told her that he was compelled to carry out his perilous scheme because he was bound in honour. It was high-flown, unpractical, Quixotic, if you wish. But—that same old Don. Was he a buffoon or a hero? Forsooth, some of us hardly know. This world of ours would be a sorry place were we all practical, and did we all fly low. And I venture to think that this man with whom we deal was no exception—there are others like him. That he is no creature of the imagination, but an honest nineteenth-century Englishman, who paid the income-tax, and sometimes wore a silk hat, can easily be ascertained, for these events are but five years old, and there are men in many London club-rooms to-day who will tell you of Claud Tyars. It is just because he is of our own time that I have attempted to string together this record in the hope

that some may read it and gather from
the study a little pride in that they claim
with such as he a joint nationality and a
co-inheritance of those strong plain virtues
which made, in days gone by, a great nation
out of a little island.

That singular sense of familiarity seemed
to have come to them again, as it had come
once before. There was no explanation,
and they yet understood each other well
enough. It seemed as if they had known
each other all their lives, almost as if they
had met in some other life. She turned
and looked across the room at him with
drawn and weary eyes in which there was
yet a smile as if to tell him that she was
strong, that he need not fear for her. And
he met her gaze with that self-suppressing
gravity. He had set bounds for himself,
and beyond these he would not step an
inch, not even for her. He would not tell

her that he loved her because, if you please, he considered it wrong to do so under the circumstances. Here was a man who not only had principles, but actually acted up to them instead of seeking to make others do so. For we all have principles applicable to the conduct of our neighbours.

"Can you tell me," he said at length, "whether this is accidental or intentional?"

"This meeting?"

"Yes."

She shook her head.

"I cannot say," she answered, loyal to her friend. She knew that if it was intentional, Agnes Winter was not the woman to do such a thing wantonly.

He answered his own question.

"It must," he said, judicially, "have been intended. Of course with every good motive—but it was a little cruel."

"She did not know," pleaded the girl.

"She did not understand. Perhaps we are not quite the same as other people."

"You are not," he answered, slowly; "there is no one like you."

It is probable that such words had been spoken to her before, for there are men—slimy parasites—who seek to raise themselves in the esteem of others by fulsome flattery, and if she had passed through a few London seasons without meeting some samples, she must have been singularly lucky. But the words were spoken so simply and with so much straightforward honesty that the veriest prude could not have taken offence. Moreover, this girl had apparently no thought of such a thing.

She glanced at him, and then her gaze fell on nothing more interesting than a somewhat ancient carpet. This was more or less appropriate, for in her dear gray eyes there was ancient history—the most

ancient of all—older than any Egyptian
record. Dreams! Nothing but dreams of
what might have been if . . . Ah, that little
word! there is no crueller in the dictionary.
If, my brethren, life were not what it
most assuredly is, we might be happy. If
human beings were only not human, there
might be bliss here below. If, moreover,
I who write these poor lines were only a
gifted novelist, I might know how to patch
things up. I might do away, not only
with the few yards of carpet that lay
between them, but with the larger, tougher
circumstances that held them apart. I
might work up a series of marvellous and
wholly impossible events, draw most heavily
upon the reserve of your credulity, and
close with the astounding untruth that
these two were happy ever after. But I
am a modest man. I am shy of taking
upon myself the task of improving the

Creator's work, of offering suggestions to the Almighty. We may rest assured that He has done the best for us possible under the circumstances. This is no work of imagination; it is merely a somewhat lame statement of facts, and if these facts are to be subverted for the edification of readers, it would be hard to know where to make the commencement.

Before either of these two persons had spoken again, their opportunity of ever doing so was taken from them, for Miss Winter was heard approaching, singing as she came. She opened the door noisily, and came into the room, rather too slowly, considering the emphasis with which the handle had been turned.

"Ah!" she exclaimed, without surprise, "you have come. It is very good of you, for Oswin tells me you are very busy."

She looked at him very keenly, but never

glanced in the direction of Helen, who was arranging some untidy music on the top of the piano.

"Yes," he answered, rather vaguely, "I have a good deal to do."

"It is," she hastened to say, in her most practical way, "about Tim—what is his name?"

"Peters?" suggested he.

"Peters—yes. You never forget anything."

"I do not forget very much," he admitted, in the same perfunctory way, but he looked over her head towards Helen, which made the quick-witted little woman of the world think that perhaps the remark was not intended for her information alone.

"A friend of mine," she continued, "a Mr. Mason, wants a boy on board his yacht, and I thought that Peters would do, if you are not taking him with you."

"No," quietly, "I am not taking him with me."

"Then I may send young Peters to see Mr. Mason?"

"Certainly. I am much obliged to you for troubling."

He was at his stiffest, and Miss Winter could not help admiring the innate good-breeding with which he attempted to seem pleasant and conversational. She had seen from the threshold that her plot had failed, and it was just one of those plots which cannot afford to fail. Success would have made her a benefactor to both, but success had not come to her, and she recognized instantly the falseness of her position. She knew this man well enough to foresee that he would never forgive her; for, as he himself had said, he was not of those who forget. She knew that this little plot, which had been hatched in a minute, and executed in ten, would alter the friendship between herself and this man during the rest of their lives. And she had always liked him; from the first she had been drawn towards him insensibly. There was something in his strong, self-contained nature that appealed to her cheery womanhood, and now she felt his anger as she had never felt the wrath of any one since her girlhood. Perhaps this feeling unnerved her. It is just possible that something might have been said or done just then which would have altered everything. There are moments when our lives hang on a balance, and in such times we cannot do better than did Claud Tyars; we cannot do better than throw boldly in the weight of duty, which is the truest weight and measure placed in our mortal hands.

Agnes Winter was fully aware that between herself and Claud Tyars no explanation would take place. He was not the sort of man to listen to or offer explanations. She knew that he would never speak of this incident, and felt that her own courage would fail her to broach the subject.

There was nothing for it but to let him go. She had been actuated by the best motives. It was not her own happiness, but that of her dearest friend for which she had schemed. She had played a bold game, and now her hand—the losing hand—lay exposed. There was nothing to do but to accept defeat. She did it as pluckily as she could, shaking hands and smiling into his grave face as he left the room.

When he was gone the two women returned to their separate occupations. Helen opened a music-book, and arranged it upon the stand, as a preliminary to seating herself at the piano.

Miss Winter had some letters to write.

She drew a little table towards the fire, and made a certain small fuss in opening ink-stand and blotting-book; but she did not commence writing, and somehow or other Helen did not begin to play. She turned the pages, and seemed uncertain as to the selection of a piece.

At last the elder woman looked up—or, to be more correct, she raised her head, and looked into the bright fire, touching her lips reflectively with the feathers of a quill pen.

" He looks worn and tired," she said.

" Yes," answered the girl, softly, and in that little word there was a whole world—a woman's world, which is a much larger thing than our world. Ours is a place wherein to work until we are tired, and then to rest until we are ready to work again. It is a place wherein a few pleasures are scattered here and there among the tasks, and some of us seem to meet with but one or two of them, while we come across a great deal of heavy labour. But women—the women at least of whom some of us cannot help writing—have little actual work set them to do. The best of them, moreover, find that pleasure fails to fill up all their time, and so they dream. They make tasks for themselves, and love to execute them carefully, for these are the labours of love. And in their leisure moments they sit down and make for themselves this larger world, which is beyond our comprehension, because our minds are necessarily full of the hard, hammer-headed facts of daily life—daily competition, and the daily struggle to wrest a livelihood out of our neighbours' pockets.

Some men there are, however, fortunate enough to form a part—perhaps the greatest part—of this unseen world to some woman; and it really matters very little that she clothe him in a wondrous individuality of her own creation. If he is true to her, and honestly endeavours to do his best by her, a higher Hand than his will see that the veil be not torn too ruthlessly from her eyes.

"All this to-do," you will say, "about a little word!" All this to-do, if you please, and infinitely more, for it was all contained in the small word spoken by this girl. It claimed possession, and even pretended to a monopoly, as if this anxiety were hers, and she were jealous of its possession; as if this man's weal or woe, his incomings, his out-goings, his words and his deeds, were hers— hers alone to sigh over, to weep, to rejoice, to despair over. And just because it was her property, she refused to discuss it, even as you and I have probably one person in the world whose virtues or faults we utterly refuse to discuss with any living soul.

CHAPTER IV.

EASTON'S CARE.

A S the middle of February approached,
Claud Tyars was tranquilly engaged
in his preparations. Several ladies were
pleased to express their disapproval of this
affectation of hard work, and failed to see
why his evenings should be devoted to a
task for which he had plenty of time during
the day. But then ladies rarely see the
necessity of complete devotion, and never
quite understand that love of work or sport
which exercises over men an absorbing influence. This is doubtless the reason why
woman's schemes grow hoary and effete in

their childhood. This is why women are still talking of their rights, and have not yet secured them. There are also, however, many men who are no better in this respect than the weaker sex—men who imagine that the larger deeds of life are done *en passant*. It takes a strong mind to compass absorption, and a stronger to battle successfully against it. In the course of our lives we occasionally meet with a mind of this description—a mind that can shake itself free at times from the absorbing pursuit, and take quite a natural interest in the smaller environments of existence. But such men are rare; and as the world goes on, gathering detail day by day, they bid fair to become extinct. It simply comes to this, that there is no time to master the entirety of more than one subject, be it work or be it play; and if we attempt to handle matters of which we are only partially masters, some one else with fuller knowledge will come and supersede us, holding us up to ridicule and contempt.

Claud Tyars did not possess one of the rare intellects cited above. I do not claim that for him. He was no genius—no *rara avis*—but merely a purposeful, somewhat stubborn Englishman, such as one may meet on any club stairs in London, at most hours of the day or night. The only remarkable thing about him was the possession of a singular memory; but as that, individually, had no direct influence upon his life, it has not been made much of in this record. The memory, as it happens, does not stand alone like some other gifts, such as music, or drawing, or a voice. It has not the power to make a man, of its own individual strength, like one of these; and yet if it be given in conjunction with some slight talent, it will raise that talent and its possessor almost to the level of genius.

It would be hard to determine how far Tyars realized his position. He was a disciplinarian of the firmest mould, and it is probable that he had never, up to this time, allowed for a moment the fact that he loved Helen Grace. This determination to cultivate the blindness of those who will not see was not dictated by cowardice; because Claud Tyars was, like most physically powerful men, inclined to exaggerate the practice of facing disagreeable facts with both eyes open. He had refused to realize this most inconvenient truth, because he was oppressed by a vague fear that realization meant betrayal. His attitude was one assumed often enough by many of us. He wished to be in a position to deny.

He was, as I have attempted to show, a fairly determined man, and one anxious to act up to slowly-conceived principles. His attitude towards Helen Grace had been, from a period previous to the fire at the Epic Theatre, a carefully-studied demonstration of indifference. And now all this had crumbled to dust ; his lofty barricade had been thrown down at the raising of a woman's hand. From the very first there had been, between himself and Agnes Winter, an antagonism of which the chief peculiarity was a marked lack of enmity. They were friends, but unquestionably antagonistic.

He now suspected that Miss Winter had known all along that Helen Grace was not the same to him as other women. Added to this was a suspicion that she calmly and deliberately undertook the task of forcing him to say as much to Helen herself. He could think this now without vanity. And there was left to him, as he quitted Miss

Winter's house, the startling knowledge that she had succeeded in her purpose. Most men, sooner or later in their lives, find themselves outwitted by a woman. It is usually in some trifling matter, and just one of those trifles which affect greater questions to follow. It was something new for Tyars to find himself in this position. He had, you see, had remarkably little to do with women, which probably accounted for this novelty.

Miss Winter's action puzzled him exceedingly. He was inexperienced, and therefore ignorant of a great motive influencing the thoughts of women all through their lives : namely, the love of Love. This is a motive of which men are singularly ignorant. Has any one ever met a male match-maker ? Has any one come across a father who is by turns conveniently blind and inconveniently keen-sighted, as are nine mothers out of ten ? Have you, my friend, ever been assisted in that little affair of yours with—you know who, by Tom or Dick or Harry ?

A French cynic (whose name is here suppressed, because his works and his sayings are so very cheap) was of opinion that a woman first loves her lover, and then loves Love. Like those of other nationalities this French cynic occasionally sacrificed truth to smartness. He oftentimes failed to deliver an epigram by endeavouring to be too epigrammatic ; and one regrets that he should at times have expressed his thought in such a few words. The old philosopher knew well enough that at the bottom of all feminine passions there is the love of Love itself.

Claud Tyars had never studied women, for the simple reason that he had never had cause to do so. It was therefore a mystery

to him why Agnes Winter should have
meddled in a matter distinctly personal to
himself. His anger against the lady was
chiefly aroused by a chivalrous respect for
the feelings of Helen Grace; and his
dominating thought during the few days
following his visit to Miss Winter, was that
he was bound in honour to avoid meeting
Helen before he sailed. But at times the
recollection of that short interview would
force its way into his mind, leaving him
irresolute. She knew now, so what difference could it make? He remembered each
little incident, each word spoken, and the
tiniest inflection of tone in the speaking.
Every movement was before his eyes, and
he was haunted by the vision of Helen,
as she stood near the fire looking back
over her shoulder at him, with a smile in
those soft, pathetic, old-world eyes of hers.
It was a smile that would haunt him

ever after ; for once his memory was a curse.

It never occurred to him to wonder over the singular lack of surprise in his own mind at his present position. Indeed there was to his simple, straightforward comprehension no cause for astonishment in the fact that he should love Helen Grace ; and many a subtler man than this athletic Briton has argued to himself that there is no surprise in love. Most men are convinced that there is no alternative. Discipline is a necessity which the majority of boys are taught to recognize before they learn anything else, and whatever it may be to women, love is a discipline to men. It seems very plain that there is for the majority of us one woman placed in the world within our reach (though many of us have to stretch up or down to meet her), and we must love that woman simply because she is there for the purpose. We may see her faults and deprecate them— these faults may clash continually with our own, but still we love her and we cannot help it. We simply bow to a necessity without defining it. It seems that all the surprise lies in the other side of the question; namely, in the fact that we are loved. But Claud Tyars was not one of those subtle persons who would distil all the joy out of life by too deep analysis. It never occurred to him to attempt a definition of Helen's feelings towards himself. He had not asked her if she could ever love him, she had told him nothing unasked; and yet it seemed to be all understood between them. It was one of those many things which go *sans dire* among us who have tongues to speak and ears to hear—one of the cases which the heart appropriates and understands with an understanding beyond

that of the ears or eyes. They had never
spoken much together, these two. They
had only met at odd moments in odd,
public places; and almost all their words
have been set down here. But there was
something else which cannot be set down
here, which never has been set on paper
yet; something which, by the mere presence or absence of a certain person, lends
a superhuman interest to trifles or deprives
existence of its charm.

These thoughts may have revolved,
flitted, chased each other through the mind
of this Englishman; but, true to his birth,
he never put them into shape: he never
attempted definition. There are many
things which cannot be defined, and the
chiefest of them I take to be a woman's
heart. There is the loftiest pride, and close
beside it the completest humility; but one
can never tell which of the two will be

up in arms before the other. With one of them most women meet most difficulties; but as far as I, in a small way, have learnt to know them, no rule can be laid down as to which arm they will take up under any circumstances that may arise.

During the few days that followed his call at Miss Winter's, Tyars avoided meeting Oswin Grace. There was plenty of work to be done, and he did it with extraordinary care, and a marked attention to detail. He heard that the younger Peters had been engaged by the yachtsman, and was to enter upon his new duties the second week in March. The old carpenter was still sore, but more resigned to being parted from his son. From the persistence with which he spoke well of Miss Winter, it appeared probable that this better state of mind had been brought about by her influence.

There was, however, one person from

whose society Tyars found it impossible to withdraw. This person was Matthew Mark Easton; the keenest observer, as it happened, among his friends. Since the receipt of Pavloski's letter the American had appeared to realize suddenly the responsibility he was incurring. There is a period in every scheme, whether it deal in peace or war, when this sudden sense of responsibility is recognized; and this period usually follows on the first action.

At all hours of the day or night Easton kept dropping in, either at the club or on board the exploring vessel. There were a thousand minor points upon which he wished to consult Tyars, a thousand trifling orders executed which had to be reported to the leader.

And he managed very cleverly. Any one with sufficient leisure and astuteness to dog the footsteps and follow out the

motives of this keen-witted American during
that chill month of February five years ago,
would have been edified by a complete
study of unobtrusive watchful care. He
never quite understood his friend ; he never
quite arrived at the inner wheels of his
mind to see that which was being slowly
ground there. But he was conscious of
the grinding, and he sometimes wondered
what sort of man Claud Tyars would be
when he had passed through this phase of
his life. Since boyhood Tyars had always
been singular. There had been no turning-
points in his life, no acute angles; but there
had been one or two great broad curves
around which as boy and as man he had
pressed with a strong slow impulse, just
as some of us have seen huge rivers like
the Nile, or the Volga, or the Danube
press onward round curve and over sunny
plain with a force which comes we know

not whence; but we can see that while it is slow and gentle, it means to go on, and there is no resisting it.

Matthew Mark Easton stood and watched, as you may have watched these slow strong rivers, and knew that his friend was passing on to some new country with a purpose which he could not stay nor turn aside. Probably he felt a little doubtful of Claud Tyars—felt that he could not rely upon him to act like other men. At any moment the unexpected might supervene.

Deeply, however, as he felt his responsibility, anxious as he was, he never lost spirit. He was one of those men whose courage rises to the occasion, and while he recognized fully that without Claud Tyars failure was inevitable, he would not blind himself into the belief that the leader was absolutely safe.

This is perhaps the time to justify as

far as possible the action of these three
men. To begin with, it must be clearly
understood that escape from Siberia by
the north is a perfectly feasible thing.
That it has been attempted by a party
of men quite inadequately prepared, almost
without money and entirely dependent on
their own resources, is an historical fact.
At least it is as historical as any fact
connected with the darker side of Russian
domestic administration. That the attempt
failed is equally well known, but success
was almost within the grasp of these
desperate fugitives, and only eluded them
by the want of such facilities as could easily
have been supplied by outside aid. That
the attempt to effect such an escape was
on another occasion crowned with success,
is a fact upon which it is inexpedient to
enlarge here. This is, partially at least,
a work of fiction, and it would be cowardly

and very despicable to endanger the liberty
of two brave men by taking advantage of
confidence, in order to claim the first telling
of their history. In anticipation therefore
of comment, and in view of shoulders
sceptically shrugged, it is perhaps wise to
deny the charge of improbability at once.
This scheme of assisting escape from the
vast prison-land of Russia by the Arctic
Ocean is not an impossible dream conceived
by the novelist in order to find a picturesque
background for his stage. For surely the
life that throbs and writhes and struggles
all around us—the life going on beneath
the thousands, nay the millions of smoking
chimneys in London, is sufficiently interesting to write about, to read of, and to
meditate upon, without inventing impossible human beings and impossible human
lives.

In reply therefore to all scepticism as

to the possibility of escape from Siberia by the north, there are only four words to say. It has been done!

In reply to arguments on the improbability of two Englishmen and an American taking up this scheme, and spending thereupon their time, their money, and their energies; risking therein their lives, their reputations, and in the case of Oswin Grace a career, it can only be pleaded that it is an easy matter to find half a dozen Englishmen ready at this moment to do the same.

And, speaking generally, as one wanders over the face of the globe, gathering evidence here and there, picking up little odds and ends of stories (the never-failing and always fresh stories of the lives of men), it seems hard to recognize that there is anything which some Englishman or another will not undertake.

CHAPTER V.

AT the risk of being accused of betraying the secrets of the sex, this opportunity is taken of recording an observation made respecting men. It is simply this, that we all turn sooner or later to some woman in our difficulties. And when a man has gone irretrievably to the dogs, his descent is explicable by the simple argument that he happened to turn to the wrong woman.

Matthew Mark Easton had hitherto got along fairly well without feminine interference, but this in no manner detracted from his respect for feminine astuteness. This respect now urged him to brush his hat very carefully one afternoon, purchase a new flower for his button-hole, and drive to Miss Winter's.

He found that lady at home and alone.

"I thought," he said, as he entered the room and placed his hat carefully on the piano, "that I should find you at home this afternoon. It is so English outside. Excuse my apparent solicitude for my hat. It is a new one. Left its predecessor at the Epic."

"The weather does not usually affect my movements," replied Miss Winter. "I am glad you came this afternoon, because I am not often to be found at home at this time."

"Oh!" he answered, coolly, as he accepted the chair she indicated. "I should have gone on coming right along till I found you in."

Easton's way of making remarks of this description sometimes made an answer superfluous, and Miss Winter took it in this light now. She laughed and said nothing, obviously waiting for him to start some new subject.

He sat quietly and looked with perfect self-possession, not at the carpet or the ceiling, as is usual on such occasions, but at her. At last it was borne in upon him that he had not called for this purpose, pleasant as the exercise of it might be; so he spoke.

"Then," he said, conversationally, " you go out mostly in the afternoons ? "

" Yes ; I am out a great deal. I have calls to make and shops to look at, and I often take tea with Helen."

His little nod seemed to say, " Yes ; I know of that friendship."

" And," he continued, with a vast display of the deepest interest, " I surmise that you

go in a close carriage, so that the weather
does not hinder you."

"No; I only have an open carriage, a
Victoria."

" Ah ! "

" It is a very convenient vehicle, so easy
of access."

" Yes ; so I should surmise."

" And it is light for the horse."

" Runs easily ? " he inquired, almost
eagerly.

" Yes, it runs easily."

Then they seemed to come to a full-stop
again. She racked her brain for some subject
of sufficient interest and not too far removed
from the safe topic of weather.

It was a ludicrous position for two
persons of their experience and *savoir-faire*.
At last Miss Winter gave way to a sudden
impulse without waiting to think to what
end the beginning might lead.

" How is Mr. Tyars ? " she asked.

" He is well," was the answer, "thank you. His arm is knitting nicely."

There was a little pause, then he added with a marked drawl (an Americanism to which he rarely gave way)—

" Ho—w is Miss Grace ? "

Agnes Winter looked up sharply. They had got there already, and her loyalty to friend and sex was up in arms. And yet she had foreseen it surely all along. She had known from the moment of his entering the room that this point was destined to be reached.

Matthew Mark Easton met the gaze of those clever northern eyes with a half smile. His own quick glance was alert and mobile. His look seemed to flit from her eyes to her lips and from her lips to her hands with a sparkling vitality impossible to follow. They seemed to be taking mental measure each of the other in friendly antagonism, like two fencers with buttoned foils.

She gave a little short laugh, half pleased, half embarrassed, like the laugh of some fair masker when she finds herself forced to lay aside her mask.

"I wonder," she said, "how much you know!"

The strange, wrinkled face fell at once into an expression of gravity which rendered it somewhat wistful and almost ludicrous.

"Nothing—I guess!"

"How much you surmise . . ." she amended, unconsciously using a word towards which he had a decided conversational penchant.

"Everything. My mind is in a fevered state of surmise."

He sat leaning forward with his arms resting on his dapper knees, with a keen, expectant look upon his nervous face. He was just a little suggestive of a monkey waiting to catch a nut.

The lady leant back in her chair meditating deeply. She was viewing her position, and perhaps remembering that her acquaintance with this man was but of three months' growth.

" Is there anything to be done ? " she asked, after a lengthened pause.

" I counted," he answered, " that I would put that question to you."

She nodded her head gravely.

" I thought perhaps that as you had come to me, you wished me to help you in something."

He looked distressed, for her meaning was obvious.

" No—I came to you . . . because . . . well, because you seemed the right person to come to."

She shrugged her shoulders.

"That is a mistake."

"Why?" he asked.

"Don't you see that I can do nothing, that I am powerless?"

He shook his head before replying tersely—

"Can't say I do. I do not know how these things are done in England, but . . ."

She interrupted him with a short laugh in which there was a noticeable ring of annoyance.

"It is not a question of how they are done in England. There can only be one way of doing it all the world over."

"And who is to do it, Miss Winter?"

"You, Mr. Easton."

"And," he continued imperturbably, "what am I to do?"

"Well . . . I should go to Mr. Tyars and say: 'Claud Tyars, you cannot go on this expedition—you have no right to sacrifice the happiness of . . . of another to the gratification of your own personal ambition.' "

" I can't do that," he said, deliberately.

" Won't," she corrected.

" Can't," he persisted, politely.

" Why ? "

" I can't tell you."

" Won't, again," she commented.

" I do not see," he argued, defending himself in anticipation, " that any one is to blame. It is an unforeseen accident ; a misfortune."

" It is a great misfortune."

" And yet," he pleaded, looking at her in a curious way, " it could not have been foreseen. We are all of us liable to such misfortunes. I had no reason to suspect that Tyars was more liable than myself. It might have happened to me."

" Yes," she answered, more softly, without raising her eyes. " Yes, it might."

He had uttered the words in such a

manner as to render the thought infinitely ludicrous. She thought that such a thing might happen to him. And yet somehow she failed to laugh. Perhaps there was an undercurrent of pathos in the thin pleasant voice, into which her thoughts had drifted.

"I cannot say," she continued, "that I foresaw it, for that was impossible. There was no time. But . . . I think I knew it the moment I saw them together, when Oswin brought him to dine at Brook Street. They had met before, some years ago, at Oxford, you know."

"Then," he said, in a relieved tone, "I surmise the matter is out of our hands."

"It never was in our hands, Mr. Easton," corrected the lady.

He looked wistfully uneasy, as if caught in the act of enunciating high treason.

"No," he said, meekly.

"Such matters are rarely in the hands of outsiders, and in those rare cases only to a very small extent."

"No—yes," he conceded with additional meekness.

In his airy way Matthew Mark Easton was a wise man. He held his peace and waited. In the expressive language of his native land, it may be said that he let the lady "have the floor." The question was one upon which he eagerly allowed his companion to have the first and longest say. He was rather awed by the proportions of it, treated generally, and by the intricacies of the individual illustration of which he formed an unwilling figure.

"I have done my best," she said, "to put a stop to this extremely foolish expedition. I notice you look surprised, Mr. Easton; that is hardly complimentary, for it would insinuate that my efforts were so puny as to have been overlooked entirely."

He denied this with an expressive gesture of the hand.

" Of course," she continued, " if men choose to risk their lives unnecessarily, I suppose there is no actual law to stop them. But they should first look round in their own home circle, and see that their lives are entirely their own to risk. Foolhardiness, entailing anxiety for others, is little short of a crime. Men lose sight of this fact very often in their desire to convince the world of their courage and enterprise. Claud Tyars ought never to have gone to Brook Street."

" But how was he to know ? "

" He knew," said the lady, deliberately, " that he loved Helen. He knew that he had loved her ever since he was a boy."

" But," argued Easton, " the fact of his loving her could scarcely be looked upon as a crime so long as he kept it to himself. Tyars is deep. I do not often know what he is driving at myself. He never asked Miss Grace to reciprocate his feelings."

Miss Winter laughed in derision.

"What have I done? I surmise I've made a joke," said Easton.

"Excuse my laughter," she said. "But you obviously know so little about it. Do you actually imagine that Helen Grace does not know, and has not known all along, that Claud Tyars looks upon her as the only woman in the world, so far as he is concerned?"

"I have hitherto imagined that, Miss Winter."

"Then you have never been in love."

He looked at her with twinkling eyes, and seemed to be on the point of saying something which, however, he never did, and she continued rather hurriedly—

" Let me warn you," she said, "against
a very common error. Men, and especially
young men, are in the habit of believing
that women evolve a love for them out of
their own inner consciousness. They go
about the world with a pleased sense of
uncertainty as to the number of maidens
who have fixed, hopelessly and unsought,
their wayward affections upon them."

Easton acknowledged the truth of this
statement by a quick nod of the head.

" You may take it," continued the lady,
" as a rule almost without exception, that
girls *never* give their love to a man unsought. The man may not speak of his
love, but he betrays it, and the result is
the same. A girl may admire a man, she
may be ready to love him, but the only
thing that can attract her love is his. I
know I am right in this, Mr. Easton. It
is the fashion to rant about the incom-

prehensibility of women, but we understand each other. If Mr. Tyars had been
indifferent to Helen she would never . . ."

She stopped, arrested by a quick movement of his hand.

"Don't!" he said, with that peculiar
deliberation which is a transatlantic demonstration of shyness ; "don't say any more
on that point. There are certain things
which we men do not like discussing."

She gave a little laugh, and changed
colour like a girl.

"I admire your chivalry," she said. "It
is genuine, and consequently rare."

"I did not know," he answered, simply,
"that it was chivalry. If it is, Miss Grace
has taught it to me. It is her due. She
reminds me of an old picture I must have
seen somewhere when I was a little chap.
Such girls must have lived in England
when we roamed in the backwoods. We

have none like them in my country. Discuss Tyars as much as you like, but do not let us talk about Miss Grace."

"I believe," said the lady, "that you are half in love with her yourself."

"No," he answered, gravely, "I am not, because . . . well, no matter—that does not count."

"I wish," Agnes Winter went on to add, in that peculiarly hurried way previously noticed, "that we knew what to do."

"I," he said, "can only tell you one thing, namely, that Claud Tyars will go on this expedition. Nothing will prevent that. Besides—he must go."

"Why?" pleaded the lady, using unscrupulously all her powers of fascination, all the persuasion of her eyes.

"I cannot tell you."

"You are as determined a man as Claud Tyars himself."

"I am, I reckon—in some things."

"Surely you can trust me, Mr. Easton."

He moved uneasily in his seat, and she, taking advantage of his hesitation, leant forward with her two hands held out in supplication ; then he seemed to yield.

"Because," he said, in an even, emotionless voice, "Claud Tyars has bound himself to go, and I will not let him off his contract! It is my expedition."

He hardly expected her to believe it, knowing Tyars and himself as she did. But he was quite aware that he laid himself open to a blow on the sorest spot in his heart.

"Then why do you not go yourself, Mr. Easton ?"

He winced under it all the same, though he made no attempt to justify himself. She had touched his pride, and there is no prouder man on earth than a high-bred

North American. He merely sat and endeavoured to keep his lips still, as Tyars would have managed to do. In a second Miss Winter saw the result of the taunt, and her generous heart was softened.

"I beg your pardon," she said; "I know there must be some good reason."

She waited in order to give him an opportunity of setting forth his good reason, but he refused to take it, and she never had the satisfaction of hearing it from his own lips.

At this moment the front-door bell gave a good old-fashioned peal in the basement, and Easton rose to his feet at once.

"I believe," he said, "that it would be inexpedient for me to be seen here by Miss Grace, or Oswin, or Tyars. They would know what we had been talking about."

Miss Winter saw the correctness of his judgment.

" Yes," she answered, " I expect it is Helen. Come into this second drawing-room. When you hear this door opened, go out of the other and down-stairs. Good-bye. Come and see me again."

" I will," he said, vanishing into the inner room.

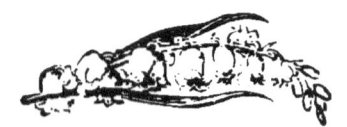

CHAPTER VI.

EASTON MAKES A STAND.

THERE is one distinct drawback to the practice of making disinterested endeavours. This lies in the simple fact that no one (not even the best of friends) believes in the motive of such endeavours. A disinterested man is like the sea-serpent, inasmuch as those who have met him are so systematically pooh-poohed that they begin to disbelieve the evidence of their own senses. A disinterested woman is still rarer, though one might find such a creature if one took the trouble to search, and lived long enough to do so systematically.

But the disinterested woman was a specimen of the human kind which had not yet come to classification in the mind of Matthew Mark Easton. He effected his retreat with masterly success, but was unfortunate enough to carry away with him a wrong impression; namely, that Miss Winter had endeavoured to frustrate his plans, not for Helen's sake, but for her own. It was not Claud Tyars whom she wished to keep in England, but Oswin Grace, and in the meantime it was very convenient to assign an impersonal reason to her antagonism. Easton thought no less of Miss Winter because she adopted this ruse. He had been reared in a keen competitive school, teaching somewhat vague scruples; and in matters of love it is well known that the line is very lightly drawn that separates the honourable from the dishonourable.

Easton was a keen analyst of the smaller

factors of daily existence. He was an expert on the surface of the human mind. Without making any great study of character, without looking very deep for motives, his knowledge of the superficial was exceedingly varied. Little conversational and social habits rarely escaped his notice. Had he been a novelist he would have recorded with infinite subtlety the small-beer of social intercourse from which is distilled the drachm of spirit called Individuality. But beyond that his powers would have been unable to reach. He could not have drawn a character with any sequence, although the same might be hidden in the unclassified mass of his chronicles. And, after all, his method had its good points. He may have made mistakes; but you may study human nature all your life, by any method whatsoever, and you will do the same. Many of us, you know, are devoid of character.

The majority of us without doubt are in this position. We (the majority) are all superficies and no depth, all small-beer and no spirit. And so the superficial method is probably the safest. One meets with more momentary motives than permanent purposes, although in many cases the former in their number tend directly or indirectly to the service of a single purpose. These cases, however, are generally women, and the gentle divergence of all small motives to one great purpose is not the force of the character, but the tendency of the soul. We may read character, but the soul is illegible. One can foretell the career of character, but no man can say whither the soul shall lead.

Easton had studied Miss Winter in his superficial way, and during the conversation just recorded he had not failed to observe the apparent care taken by her to avoid

mentioning the name of Oswin Grace. Some
astute readers may think that there was a
reason for this keen-sightedness. Perhaps
it was so, but that will be seen hereafter.
And in anticipation of possible criticism
it may be well to recognize now the probability that some may think these people
too subtle in their motives, too secret, too
much given to concealment to be quite
natural. Some may opine that there are too
many cross purposes and crooked answers
in this narration to be quite true to life.
But it is this very truth that makes it so,
for this is no flight of poesy, no idyll of the
nineteenth century, but a plain record of
such incidents as influenced the lives of
certain people, some of whom will read this
page, while others have learnt the meaning
of it all; and, having received understanding,
are aware of those flaws in mortal life which
make existence what it is. And in self-

defence let me ask you if *you* have never
played this same game of cross purposes
and crooked answers. Let me ask if you
and your friends are in the habit of boldly
publishing the inward thoughts of your
hearts in order to save others from harbour-
ing error—if you have met a maiden willing
to expose the inward secret of her soul in
order to save others from mistakes. It is
a fruitful topic, this one of mistakes, and
some day I shall write an astounding essay
upon it for an influential magazine, when
requested to do so by its editor. Without
mistakes the world would be a very different
place from what it is. Looking at it from
a political economical point of view this
state of infallibility would be most dis-
astrous, for the labour-market would be
overstocked even more than it is at present.
In every bank, in all large offices, are there
not a number of clerks whose sole duty is

to seek for and correct the mistakes of others? And contemplating it from a social standpoint, many of us would find time hanging very heavily on our hands had we not such fruitful employment in the correction of our own mistakes, the patching up of our own blunders, the elucidating of our own muddles.

Matthew Mark Easton was a quick thinker if not a deep one, and it is those who think quickly who give quickly. This man had something to give, something to tear away from his own heart and hold out with generous smiling eyes, and before Miss Winter's door had closed behind him the sacrifice was made. He called a hansom-cab and drove straight to Tyars' club. He found his friend at work among his ship's papers, folding and making up in packets his receipted bills.

"Morning," said the Englishman. "These

papers are almost ready to be handed over
to you.   All my stores are on board!"

"Ah!"

Tyars looked up sharply, and as sharply
returned to his occupation.   Easton was
grave—an unusual occurrence, and Tyars
knew that he had come with news of some
sort.   He waited, however, for the American
to begin, and continued to fold and arrange
his papers.

"I have," said Easton, sitting down
and tapping the neat toe of his boot with
his cane, "hit quite accidentally upon a
discovery . . ."

"Poor chap!" muttered Tyars, abstractedly.

"Which will make a difference in your
crew."

"What?" exclaimed Tyars, pausing in
the middle of a knot.

"One rule," continued Easton, his queer
little face twisting and twinkling with some

emotion, which he was endeavouring to conceal, " was that no sweethearts or wives were to be left behind."

" What are you driving at ? " asked Tyars, curtly, in a singularly lifeless voice.

He was studying a long ship-chandler's bill with the keenness of an accountant.

" I surmise that my recollection of that rule is correct."

" I suppose so."

" Well—" Easton paused. " Well, old man, I have discovered a sweetheart."

" Don't be an ass ! "

There was something in the tone of his voice that caused Easton to glance at him keenly and then drop entirely the semi-bantering manner and assume one of the utmost gravity.

" I objected to Grace at first," he said, " because he had too many women-folk about him."

Tyars threw the papers in a heap and rose suddenly from his seat. He walked to the mantel-piece and selected a cigarette from a tin box standing there.

"Of course," he said, striking a match, "your discovery can only relate to one person."

"Yes; you know whom I mean."

Tyars nodded his head in acquiescence and continued smoking. The little American sat looking in a curious way at this large, impassive, high-bred Englishman, as if gathering enjoyment and edification from the study of him.

"Well," he drawled at length, "you say nothing!"

"There is nothing to say."

"On the contrary," returned Easton, "there is everything to say. That is one of the great mistakes made by you English people. I have noticed it since I have been in this country. You take too much for granted. You let things say themselves too much, and you think it very fine to be impassive and apparently indifferent. But it is not a fine thing, it is silly and unbusiness-like. Do you give up Oswin Grace?"

"Certainly; if you can get him to stay behind."

"Ya—as; he is another Englishman. He will run his head against a wall if he can. That is to say if there is a thick enough wall around."

Tyars laughed, and turned to flip his cigarette-ash into the fire.

"I have tried," he said, "to make him give it up."

Easton looked up in surprise.

"Indeed! upon what grounds?"

"Upon the grounds that he had ties at home which rendered him unfit for such service."

"Sister?" inquired the American.

"Yes"—slowly—"sister."

There was a little pause, and then Easton said thoughtfully—

"It is remarkable how much stronger an argument somebody else's sister is in these cases."

"U—m," opined Tyars, somewhat indifferently. He evidently did not know much about the matter.

"What did Grace say?" inquired the American, calmly.

"Oh, I don't know. He turned very white about the cheeks, and was evidently in a desperate fright."

"I suppose—he is a good man. The man you want?"

"Yes; he is the man I want."

Easton meditated for a few moments.

"And still you will give him up?"

"Yes; there are plenty of men to be had."

"Tyars, will you speak to him again," said Easton, rising and taking up his hat, "and use . . . that other argument?"

Tyars hesitated. "I am not quite sure that it is my business," he said. "I hate meddling in other people's affairs, and after all I suppose Grace knows best what he is doing."

"Men rarely know what they are doing under these circumstances," observed Easton.

He waited patiently, hat in hand, to hear what Tyars had to say. While he stood there, Muggins, the bull-terrier, rose from the hearthrug, stretched himself, and looked from one to the other in an inquiring and anticipatory manner. He took it to be a question of going for a walk, and apparently imagined that the casting vote was his.

"All right," said Tyars, suddenly, "I will speak to him again!"

"To-day," pursued Easton, following up

his advantage, " or to - morrow at the latest."

" Yes ; to-morrow at the latest."

Then the American took his departure, and Muggins curled himself up on the hearthrug again with a yawn of disappointment.

There are moments in the lives of most men when they feel themselves impelled by some vague instinct to seek advice. It does not by any means follow that they are prepared to be guided by such advice, nor are these occasions invariably critical. Indeed most men make the greater decisions of their lives quite alone, seeking the advice of none, following no example. But in the minor crises of existence, and more especially in regard to matters affecting others more than ourselves, the instinctive gregariousness of our nature asserts itself.

Claud Tyars admired Miss Winter more

than he admired any woman. The power
of her clear practical intellect was full of
fascination for him, and she was the woman
he would have chosen to consult in such
questions as men habitually consult women.
In this case it happened that she was just
the one person whose advice it was impossible to seek. Helen Grace could have
counselled him wisely and sweetly, but for
reasons of his own he set aside unhesitat-
ingly the idea of questioning her, and he
knew that she would never proffer advice
unasked.

This man was, as he had told Helen
Grace, quite alone in the world. Coming as
he did from a solitude-loving stock, he was
placed in that grade of life to which
solitude is most readily obtainable. The
upper middle-class gentleman of England
lives a larger portion of his life alone than
almost any class of men on earth. Those

above him are usually forced by their rank
to occupy positions of prominence in the
world, are therefore public servants, and
consequently at the public beck and call.
Those beneath him are not rich enough to
purchase solitude. They live in small
houses surrounded by wife and children,
within call of the servants, and not beyond
the smell of cooking.

Since meeting Matthew Mark Easton,
Tyars had withdrawn himself from society
gently and persistently, with the view of
furthering his Quixotic scheme, and in this
project circumstances were again favourable
to him. He occupied that safe retreat
between the haunt of the insupportable
society journalist and the kind-hearted
curiosity of the bourgeois. In all large
communities the art of "doing without" is
highly cultivated. It is only in very small
circles and in Scotch song-books that people

are missed for longer than a few days. It is a great pity that we have such difficulty in recognizing our own unimportance. If we did so we should be much more independent and study our own inclinations before the consideration of feelings erroneously supposed to exist in the hearts of our friends and relations.

Claud Tyars was never missed, and to do him justice he was supremely indifferent on this point. It was only at odd moments on shore when he happened to be idle during some rare periods that he gave any thought to the loneliness of his life. And in one respect he was essentially British : namely, in the calm readiness with which he undertook to settle all questions for himself. When these questions affected his fellow-men he rarely saw reason to hesitate, for most Englishmen learn as soon as they leave the nursery what is right and what is wrong; what is gentlemanly and what the reverse. But this knowledge from its source can only serve as a guide to conduct in regard to men. At the period when it is really instilled, namely, during the first few years at school, woman occupies a remarkably obscure position in the youthful mind. At no time of man's life is woman so unimportant, and therefore the boy learns and only cares to learn behaviour towards his fellow-men; moreover, that which he then learns will go with him through all the fair weather and the foul, through all the storm, and through what little sunshine there may be, till the evening of his life, and the glow of it will linger over his memory as the hushed glow of sunset lingers over a fading landscape and gives it character.

It is only later in life that we learn our manners, our bows and smirks, our entrances upon and exits from the broader stage of existence. It is then that we awaken to the truth that while men may be served with honesty, women must be treated with chivalry. At the same time we find out that chivalry and honesty are not akin, nor near thereto. It is not always kind to be honest, and if any man hesitate in the choice, let him be chivalrous and he will scarcely rue it.

Claud Tyars had not learnt chivalry at the best school, his mother's knee, for he had never stood there, and it was therefore no subtle superficial acquirement, but the honest instinctive love of fair play between strong and weak that prompted him to accede to Easton's request.

CHAPTER VII.

AND TYARS MAKES AN EFFORT.

LIKE most persons living and acting alone —gathering as it were with their own hands the harvest of their own seed—Claud Tyars was remarkable for quickness of action. Having once determined to make another effort to rid himself of his invaluable lieutenant, he lost no time in putting his thoughts into deeds. In an hour's time he was clambering up the smartly-painted side of the exploring ship *Argo*. It happened to be raining hard—the first tepid rain of spring, a few weeks in advance of the calendar—and he was clad in a long oilskin coat of which one sleeve hung limp, for his arm was not yet sufficiently healed to bear movement. Perhaps these facts accounted for a certain slowness of gait amounting almost to reluctance as he walked aft towards the companion. He groped his way down the little twisting steps with a clatter of strong boots on the brass-bound tread.

Oswin Grace was seated in the bright little cabin at a table writing out lists of stores. Many of these same stores were piled on the deck around him, and there was a pleasant odour of paraffin-oil in the air.

" Morning, old man ! " he said abstractedly, drawing the scattered papers towards himself in a heap so as to make more room on the table. At times Oswin Grace felt almost familiar with his self-contained chief.

" Good morning," answered Tyars.

He turned to hang up his gleaming oilskin on a hook just outside the cabin-door, then came back drawing off his wet gloves, which he presently threw down on the deck in front of an eager little copper stove. There was already a sense of homeliness in the manner with which the two men lived and moved and had their being in this little cabin, and Tyars suddenly became conscious of this. He suddenly realized that the cabin, the ship, his whole existence would not be quite the same without the companionship of this broad-shouldered little English sailor. He suddenly became aware of the perfect harmony existing between himself and the man who had given up an honourable career to follow him. Perhaps he caught a passing gleam of light from the other's soul, and saw for a moment into the heart of Oswin Grace, understanding the difficulties that lay hidden there. Sometimes these little glimpses of life from another point of view are vouchsafed to us, and we hover on the brink of seeing ourselves as others see us. Perhaps Claud Tyars recognized then the great difficulty attached to the occupation of a subordinate position, especially in subordination to a man like himself. An incompetent second-fiddler may make matters extremely inharmonious. Tyars leant over the table and examined one or two accounts in a desultory manner.

"Grace!" he said.

"*Adsum*," replied his companion, cheerfully, without ceasing his work.

Tyars closed the cabin-door with his elbow.

"I do not see," he said, slowly and uncomfortably, "how you can very well go with us."

Grace laid aside his pen and raised his keen gray eyes. His brow was wrinkled, his lips set, his eyes full of fight.

Tyars hesitated, and the two Englishmen remained thus for some seconds, each reading the thoughts of the other as best he might, and very imperfectly at the best.

"Because," suggested Grace in a hard voice, "I am in love with Agnes Winter?"

Tyars nodded his head and stooped to pick up his gloves, holding them subsequently close to the bars of the stove, where they steamed gaily. There was a silence of some duration, and every second increased the discomfort of Claud Tyars.

"And you," continued Grace at length very deliberately, "love Helen!"

Tyars stood upright so that his head was very near the beams. He thrust his gloves into his pocket and stood for some seconds grasping his short pointed beard meditatively with his uninjured hand.

"Yes," he said, "I do."

Grace returned to his ship-chandler's bills with the air of a barrister who, having established his point, thinks it prudent to allow time for it to sink into the brains of judge and jury.

"I do not mind telling you," he added carelessly, almost too carelessly, "that Miss Winter—is perfectly indifferent on the subject."

"Do you know that for certain?" asked Tyars, sharply.

"She told me so herself," answered Grace, with a peculiar little laugh which was not pleasant to the ear.

He waited obviously for a reciprocal confidence on the part of Tyars, but he waited in vain. The habit of non-communicativeness is one of very quick growth and its roots are deep. The silence of Oswin Grace asked as distinctly as words could have

done, 'Is Helen as indifferent as Agnes
Winter?'—and Tyars was conscious of the
question. He even made an effort to tear
down the barrier that fenced his heart round,
but an old habit is a strong antagonist. He
could not overcome that deep-seated dislike
to the discussion of all things appertaining
to thoughts or feelings, which is so characteristic of the Anglo-Saxon race. But he
tacitly abandoned all attempts then and
for ever to induce Oswin Grace to relinquish
his purpose. It was a tame ending to all
his resolutions, but his hands were tied, the
wind was knocked out of his sails, the tables
were turned upon him.

Claud Tyars was not one of those fatuous
young men who imagine that they can
conceal anything for very long from the
world. But he had hitherto been under the
impression that his love for Helen Grace was
a matter known only to himself and Helen,

suspected only by Miss Winter. And after all, if a man makes a point of avoiding entirely the woman he loves, and thus does away with the danger of betraying himself in her presence by manner, speech, or silence, he is assuredly justified in priding himself on the security of his secret. Tyars could tell on the fingers of his two hands the number of times he had spoken to Helen Grace since his return to England, and one hand would suffice to numerate the interviews which had taken place in the presence of Oswin. It is possible that in the elaboration of his plans for concealing his love from Helen herself and keeping it hidden from the keen eyes of Miss Winter and Matthew Mark Easton, he had overlooked the man who, while quietly working at his side, was acquiring a fuller cognizance of his plans, and hopes, and fears than that possessed by the American himself. This was very likely, because it is a mistake we make every day of our lives. We are always looking into distances and neglecting that which is near at hand.

Oswin Grace was the first to speak, quietly shelving his own affairs with that philosophy of resignation which is best understood by those who have been brought to manhood under discipline.

"Of course," he said, "I have no desire to meddle with your affairs. I ask no questions, and I look for no spontaneous confidences. It will be better for you to lose sight altogether of the coincidence that I am—her brother."

Tyars had seated himself on the corner of the cabin-table, with his back half turned towards his companion. He had picked up a piece of straw, of which there was a quantity lying on table and floor, and this he was biting meditatively. It was as yet entirely a puzzle to him, and this was only a new complication. He could not understand it, just as better men than Claud Tyars have failed to understand it all through. For no one, I take it, does understand love, and no man can say whither it will lead.

"There need," continued Oswin Grace, perforating a series of small holes in his blotting-paper with the point of a cedar-wood pencil, "be no nonsense of that sort. I am not going to take it upon myself to watch over Helen's interests; they are much safer in your hands than in mine."

Still Tyars said nothing, and after a little pause Grace went on in measured, thoughtful tones, carrying with them the weight of deliberation.

"There is one point," he said, "upon which I think there must be an understanding."

"Yes," said Tyars, anxiously.

"Any risks—extra risks, such as boat-work, night-work up aloft—these must be mine. From what you have said I gather that your intention was to be skipper, and yet do the rough work as well. When any-thing hazardous is to be done, I shall do it. You must stick to the ship."

The big man gave a little annoyed laugh.

"It is your duty not only towards—her, but towards the rest of us. A skipper has no right to risk his life if he can get some one of less value to risk his."

"I am not aware of any intention to deprive you of your share of the dirty work."

"You are not *conscious* of it, you mean, old fellow!" corrected Grace, "but I am. I have been conscious of it all along. I have got my knife into you now, and if you do not submit I shall woggle it about and cause you some discomfort."

The words were spoken pleasantly, almost playfully; but Tyars turned in some vague astonishment to look at his companion, and saw a look in the keen gray eyes which he had not perceived there since Oswin Grace took command of the *Martial* over his head. It was not defiance, for English eyes do not look defiance except in books; but it breathed that high-born quiet determination which knows exactly where to draw the line between discipline and servitude.

Tyars laughed and turned away his glance. It was a bold stroke, and Oswin Grace had dealt it diplomatically; for the feeling of tension that had been in the atmosphere of the little cabin seemed to relax, and a fuller understanding crept in between the two men.

"I have no doubt," said Tyars, seating himself at the table and beginning to open his letters, "that we are all constructing a

very fine mountain out of materials intended
for a mole-hill. I for one have no intention
of leaving my bones in the far North.
There is no reason why we should not all
be back home by this time next year."

"None at all," agreed Oswin, somewhat
perfunctorily, adding with a suspicion of
doubt the next minute, "Suppose we
succeed ? "

" Well, what then ? "

" Suppose we get there all right, rescue
the men and go on safely ; we get over the
elemental danger, and then we have to face
the political, which is worse."

" I do not see it," replied Tyars. " We
sell the ship at San Francisco. Half the
crew expect to be paid off there, the other
half will disperse with their passage-money
in their pockets, and very few of them will
find their way back to England. Our
doctor is a German Socialist, with several

aliases; our second mate a simple-minded
Norwegian whaling-skipper. The exiles do
not know a word of English, or pretend
they do not, and none of the crew speak
Russian. There will be absolutely no intercourse on board, and only you, the doctor,
and myself will ever know who the rescued
men really are. The crew will imagine
that they are the survivors of a Russian
ivory-hunting expedition, and if the truth
ever comes out it will be impossible to
prove that you and I knew better."

"But it will not be easy to keep the
newspapers quiet."

"We shall not attempt to keep them
quiet. It will only be a local matter. The
San Francisco papers will publish libellous
woodcuts of our countenances and a column
or two purporting to be biographical, but
the world will be little the wiser. In
America such matters are interesting only

in so much as they are personal, and there
is in reality nothing easier than the suppression of one's personality. There is no
difficulty in kicking an interviewer out of
the room, just as one would kick out any
intruder; and we are quite indifferent as to
whether the American newspapers abuse us
or not after having been kicked. As to
the details of the voyage, I shall withhold
those with the view of publishing a book,
which is quite the correct thing to do
nowadays. The book shall always be in
course of preparation, and will never
appear."

In this wise the two men continued talking, planning, scheming, all the morning,
while they worked methodically and prosaic-
ally. Whatever mistakes they may have
made, however Quixotic they may have
been, there was no fault to find in the
manner in which they fitted up their ship

and mapped out each detail of their expedition. Whatever else they may have been, they were good sailors ; and that is sufficient praise for most men.

They carefully confined their conversation to the future, and avoided all reference to those subjects which had been so lamely and scrappily discussed earlier in the day. Having set their hands to the plough, they seemed, alike, nervously determined to look always ahead, ignoring and quelling all thought of what they were leaving behind them.

CHAPTER VIII.

THE ELEVENTH OF MARCH.

EVEN the watched pot boils in time. There comes an end to all things. The painter finally lays aside his brush ; the writer at last presses his blotting-paper over " Finis." The composer must some day dot in the last chord to his opera. And these men in reaching the close of their labour complete an era of their lives. The printer also sets up " Finis " in his type, but that action is no item in his existence. It is only the end of a creation that leaves its mark upon the heart ;—it is only those who create who lose something when their work is done—who pass on in life with a sense of vacancy somewhere in their being. For that creation, whether it be picture, book, or opus, is part of the man ; it has the scent and impress of his Soul, and from his Soul a portion of its virtue has gone out.   And yet the completed work is always *there*— the creator is always conscious of its presence, of its companionship in the world —though it stand neglected on a shelf, or hang unseen in a picture-seller's back shop.

Men who have conceived and have finally brought to completion some great scheme are partakers in this feeling. They too know the joy of creation—perhaps they taste the sweetness of success. It is to be hoped that they do, because success is their guiding-star ; it is more necessary to them than to the artist, who finds joy in the act of producing alone.

Matthew Mark Easton did not claim for

his scheme the magnitude of a life-long dream. It had been conceived in idleness, and of leisure it was the fruit. But he had lived with it night and day for nearly three years, until he had fallen into the habit of thinking of little else. He had acquired that lamentable custom of looking on men and things from one point of view only— taking interest or feeling indifference in both only as possible factors. But he was unconscious of it all. Like most eloquent men he was ignorant of the distance that he might carry others by his words, and remain unmoved himself. He had carried Claud Tyars, who in turn had dragged him after, not by eloquence, but by the silent force of an absorbed will.

When Easton woke up on the eleventh morning of March he was conscious of a certain unsteadiness of purpose in minor matters. He failed to dress himself with

the quick completeness which usually characterized his toilet. He meditated over his
ablutions and dawdled with his razor. His
hand was not only slow, but distinctly
shaky, and he came very near to bloodshed.
He stepped to the window and contemplated
the heavens of a pearly green—such as goes
by the name of blue sky in London—and
this was a man who never displayed the
slightest interest in barometrical matters.

This day, the eleventh of March, was
fixed for the sailing of the *Argo* exploring
vessel, and Easton's chief thought on the
subject was a vague wonder as to what
he would do with himself after she had
gone. This little man rather prided himself
upon the possession of a hard and impreg-
nable nineteenth-century heart. He took a
certain small pleasure in the reflection that
he was as nearly independent as it is possible for any human being to be. Although

he was naturally of a gregarious and sociable habit, he held in reserve the thought that the practice of sociability was with him merely a matter of expediency, and not of necessity as it is with some. He could drop all his acquaintances at a moment's notice and never feel the loss. In fact he had of late cherished the idea of going to San Francisco to await the arrival of the *Argo*. He at all events was sanguine of success.

And yet he was distinctly disturbed this morning of the eleventh of March—disturbed, that is to say, for a man devoid of human tie or sympathy. It is possible that he was surprised at himself, and perhaps annoyed, for he whistled persistently and somewhat aggressively while he dressed.

The *Argo* was to pass out of the tidal basin into the river at one o'clock, and at half-past twelve Easton drove up to the

dock-gates.   He brought with him the last
items of the ship's outfit in the shape of a
pile of newspapers, and a bunch of hot-
house roses for the cabin-table, for there
was to be a luncheon-party on board while
steaming down the river.

He found Admiral Grace strolling about
the deck with Tyars, conversing in quite a
friendly way, and endeavouring honestly to
suppress his contempt for seamanship of so
young a growth as that of his companion.
The ladies were below, inspecting the ship
under Oswin's guidance.

The little vessel lay snugly under the
high stone quay, and presented the appearance of some quaint, old-fashioned little
man-of-war, so spotless were her decks, so
mathematically correct the coiling of every
rope, so bright her brass-work.   One could
have guessed that her first officer had served
under the white ensign.

A few idlers stood on the quay with that peaceful sense of contemplation which comes to men who pass their lives near water, and exchanged gruff monosyllables of approval at long and uncertain intervals; varying the same with an interchange of quids, and sociable expectoration.

Easton joined the two sailors after having dropped the roses and newspapers through the open cabin-skylight, and his presence was somewhat of a relief to both.

" She is," he said, addressing himself to the admiral with transatlantic courtesy, " a strange mixture of the man-of-war and the yacht—do you not find it so, sir ? "

" She is," answered the old gentleman, guardedly, " one of the most complete vessels I have ever boarded—though her outward appearance is of course against her."

" One can detect," continued the American,

looking round with a musing eye, "the influence of a naval officer."

The old gentleman softened visibly. He had been guilty of allowing it to be understood by several of his friends that his son Oswin was virtually in command of this vessel, while Claud Tyars was merely the leader of the expedition. The remembrance of this lapse had been brought back rather rudely to his conscience during the short colloquy that had been interrupted by the advent of Easton, and the admiral was just beginning to smart under a realization of Oswin's comparative unimportance. This impression had certainly not been conveyed with intention, for Tyars was perfectly ignorant of its existence. The simple truth was that he was a commander by nature, while Oswin Grace was cast in a different mould. The naval officer was an excellent subordinate, and in order to excel in this

difficult line it is essential to appear unimportant. The value of a good subordinate
should be known alone to his immediate
superior—the general public should be
unsuspicious of his worth. This was
precisely the position of Oswin Grace, and
looking at it from a naval point of view,
it was not untinged with humiliation.
Contemplated from a common-sense standpoint it could scarcely have been improved
upon ; but old gentlemen (like young
ones) do not always take this point of
view.

"Even to a landlubber like myself," said
Easton glibly, "that influence is apparent."

At this moment the ladies appeared,
escorted by Oswin Grace—Miss Winter
first, with a searching little smile in her
eyes. Easton saw that she was very much
on the alert.

"I feel quite at home," she said to him,

looking round her, "although there are so many changes."

"So do I; the more so because the changes have been made under my own directions."

They walked aft, leaving the rest of the party standing together. As they walked Oswin Grace watched them with a singular light in his clear gray eyes, singular because gray eyes rarely glisten, they only darken at times. Miss Winter and her companion, in silence, watched the pier-head hand cast off the last hawser—the last link between the *Argo* and terra-firma. It happened that the rest of the party were doing the same in a mechanically interested way.

"Does she seem to you," asked Easton, suddenly, "like an unfortunate ship?"

The Gravesend pilot who was standing near to them shouted some instructions to the master of the tug in such stentorian tones that Miss Winter was compelled to wait a few moments until he had finished his observations.

As she answered, the paddles of the tug revolved with a splash; the tow-rope seethed out of the water, and the *Argo* moved perceptibly.

" No," she answered, " there is a re-assuring air of—of something stronger than *savoir-faire* about the ship which I like."

" *Savoir-faire,*" he suggested, " not only *savoir-dire.*"

" Yes," she answered, with a comprehensive little nod; and they stood watching the tactics of the ship's crew and the dock-hands without understanding very much.

Oswin Grace had gone forward on to the diminutive old-fashioned forecastle. Claud Tyars stood beside the pilot, while the whaling-captain was not far off. There was singularly little shouting. Tyars and

Grace never opened their lips. Once Tyars made a little movement with his hand which was rotatory in its tendency. Grace answered with a nod, and spoke quietly to a man beside him, who immediately set a small steam-winch to work. For some moments there was no sound except the convulsive grunts of the winch, and these were finally arrested by a motion of Tyars' hand. These two men had slept the night before in the West End of London; they had put on their clothes there a few hours before, and in the way in which they wore these clothes (by no means maritime in cut) there was that ineffaceable stamp of the British sportsman with which one comes into contact in many strange places.

Presently the vessel glided smoothly between the slimy gates out into the open river. The tow-line was cast off, and the *Argo's* engines started. The vessel swung slowly round on the greasy waters, pointing her blunt stubborn prow down the misty river. She settled to her work with a docile readiness, like a farmer's mare on the outward road.

" This is a new experience for you," said Easton, with the faint American tinge which came to his tongue in unguarded moments.

" Yes," Miss Winter answered, " I did not want to come."

" Ah ! "—he looked up aloft where a boy was at work on a tiny yard-arm. She did not however continue, so he encouraged her. " Why did you not want to come ? "

" I knew we should be horribly in the way. I am always conscious of being in the way on a ship that is not securely tied down all round—moored, I mean."

" I do not detect any signs of annoyance on the part of the—executive."

" No," admitted Miss Winter. " One

would say that it had all been carefully rehearsed."

"Then what is the true reason?" he inquired, coolly—almost too coolly for a man of his temperament.

"I do not know. I am nervous. I dislike the dramatic . . ."

"The unrehearsed?" he suggested.

She gave a little laugh and turned away to look at a brown-sailed barge which was scudding across the river astern of them.

"Yes, the unrehearsed."

"But," he said, "there is no drama. We are a light-comedy company. We make nice little jokes and laugh at them enthusiastically. I surmise, at least, that we shall do so. The corners of my mouth are beginning to turn up already."

"I came on board," said Miss Winter, gravely, "with a broad smile which I expected to last me all day, but it appears to have faded."

He looked at her critically in his peculiar twinkling way, not untinged however with concern.

"Yes," he admitted, "it has. You must polish it up for luncheon. I intend to be intensely funny, and I guess you will have to laugh."

"I suppose Mr. Tyars will be of no assistance."

"Not of the very smallest. He is not good at that sort of thing—deep people, I take it, never are; it is only shallow water that sparkles in a breeze."

"I am still of opinion that it is a pity we came," said the lady, making a little movement to join the other group. Perhaps she was conscious of Oswin's occasional glances in her direction, but if she was there was nothing in her manner to betray it.

"I always was of that opinion," admitted the American, following her, "but I could not prevent it."

Then they joined Admiral Grace and Helen. Presently, and before any conversation had passed, Tyars and Oswin came up together. Helen was standing slightly apart, and the delicately-embarrassed interest which she was still showing in everything, was not the strangeness of a landswoman to all things maritime ; it was a new-born shyness which she could not have defined herself—a sudden maidenly fear of betraying too great an interest in any one man, or the handiwork of any one man. Whatever it may have been, it lent an additional fascination to her grave young face, for the controlled shyness of a man or woman is always pleasant to meet. To Helen Grace it was infinitely becoming, it suggested in some subtle way the glow of youth, the fresh savour of inexperience. She must have looked like that at her first ball, when gaslight had no suggestion of its native coal; when smiles were only smiles, and never masks; when she had been happy to take the surface of things.

Tyars approached her, and stood by her side with that grave attention which a pre-occupied man accords to those women who command his respect. Then suddenly, in his abrupt way, he spoke.

"You will never see this ship again," he said.

She made a little movement with her head and throat, as if a sudden chill had caused her to shiver.

"What do you mean?"

"We are going to sell her out there—at San Francisco."

"Ah—yes," she murmured with evident relief.

The effort to talk of commonplace matters in a commonplace way was a trifle *en évidence* on both sides.

"Do you admire the ship?" he asked, looking steadily at her as one looks at one's partner when the game hangs on a balance. "What is your opinion of her?"

The girl made an effort.

"Oh," she replied with a clear, firm smile, "of course I know nothing about it; but my first impression was surprise at her diminutiveness. She still seems to me absurdly small. I am woefully ignorant on nautical matters, and size appeals to me as safety."

"In this case size has little to do with safety. In fact, the smaller we are the stronger we shall be as long as we can carry all we wish. We have sent on our coal, you know, by another steamer."

"To wait for you?"

" Yes, to wait for me—for us."

It was a foolish mistake to make, but it was just one of those mistakes which the tongue sometimes takes it upon itself to perpetrate, and the brain, however alert it may be, is for the moment paralyzed.   It is a dangerous pastime to think of one thing and to talk of another.   Some of us pride ourselves that we can keep up one conversation and listen to another at the same time.

Claud Tyars had been talking with his brain while his tongue was listening to his heart; and it was singular how complete his betrayal was.   So small a slip might easily have passed unnoticed, but before he had even time to alter the pronoun Helen changed colour.   He heard the quick, gasping breath, and although he did not dare to look in her direction, he was conscious of her quickly-averted face.

Taking into consideration the social experience they must both have possessed—considering that they had danced together eight years before — they were singularly *gauches*. They did a very unwise thing ; they allowed the incident to be magnified into a silence — one of those horrid silences which come in times of pressure, when there is a strain in the atmosphere.

Parting words may be very sad, very weighty, very eloquent, but they are infinitely kinder than parting silences. Which think you to be more weighty ; the few broken words of a dying man — the recommendations, the instructions, the advice —or the breathless silence when he sinks back on the weary pillow, and in the concentration of his eyes one can read all that is unsaid—all that is never said in this world, and for which there can be no need in the next? It was Claud Tyars who finally spoke.

"Come," he said with a peculiar twisted smile; "luncheon is ready. Let us lead the way, and the others will follow."

CHAPTER IX.

OFF !

HAD an acute but uninitiated observer been introduced into the little cabin of the *Argo* during the consumption of the delicate repast provided by her officers, he or she could scarcely have failed to notice a certain recklessness of hilarity among the party assembled. Admiral Grace was the only one who really did justice to the steward's maiden and supreme effort, and he in consequence was singular in failing to appreciate the witticisms of Matthew Mark Easton and Oswin Grace. This was perhaps

owing to the fact that when we have passed
the half-way milestone in life we fail to
appreciate the most brilliant conversation if
it be served up with savoury viands and
choice wine. This, I say, was perhaps the
reason ; for we cannot always tell how much
silent old gentlemen see and note while
enjoying the fullest flavour of their sherry.
It is just possible that Admiral Grace did
not think very much of the wit—taken as
wit pure and simple. His position was not
unique. You and I, *mon vieux*, know perhaps
something about it. We also may have
found ourselves in the midst of a party of
young people who seem to have an object in
attempting very lamely to deceive each other.
We also may have listened to very feeble
witticisms recognized by silvery laughter
that follows too quickly on the heels of the
sally to be natural, and we also may have
turned philosophically to the *menu* with

a feeling that something was going on—
something vague and subtle, fit only for
young minds to understand.

Once or twice Easton's words recurred to
Miss Winter: "I intend to be intensely
funny, and I guess you will have to laugh."
This was her cue, and she acted up to it.

On the finite principle the meal came to
an end also, and a move was made. There
was nothing else to do but to go on deck,
which was not so unpleasant a resort as it
might have been with an east wind. The
admiral and Easton were accommodated
with cigars, the ladies with deck-chairs,
under the friendly cover of a windsail.
There happened to be very few steamers
going down the river, and the *Argo* glided
forward on the unctuously moving water
with that semi-helpless clumsiness which
characterizes the movement of a steamer
on the bosom of a strong tide. In certain

reaches of the river they were quite alone, and only at times they passed a Medway sailing-barge floating down to Sheerness. Occasionally a bluff weather-beaten fish-carrier or a tall-funnelled tug would steam busily past them, up-stream; but for the time all the ocean traffic seemed to be suspended. Doubtless the inward-bound liners were lying miles below, at Gravesend, conscious of having missed a tide. The denser forest of tall chimneys had been left behind, and only at intervals was either bank disfigured by slow smoking monuments of industry. The left bank lay low and dank, while to the right the watershed of Kent began already to rise in tree-covered slopes.

"Where are we?" asked Miss Winter, with a certain determined cheerfulness.

It was Tyars who answered.

"We have passed Greenwich and Woolwich; over there is Plumstead Marsh."

Miss Winter followed the direction of his outstretched hand. She belonged to the essentially sedentary circle of the West End of London, and to her Woolwich and Greenwich were merely names; the one connected with an arsenal, the other with a bygone custom of dining on a simple little fish. To her such names at Cubitt Town, Plumstead, Rainham, and Purfleet were totally unknown. There was a little silence during which both ladies looked around them with simulated interest. Tyars seemed to divine an unasked question.

"Over there is Gravesend. It is just behind that high land. The smoke you see there is from the town; we shall be there in an hour," he said.

"And do you stop—anchor, or whatever it is?" inquired Miss Winter, looking away from Helen with an almost noticeable persistence.

"No — we go on — to sea — to-night," Tyars answered crisply, with a quick glance in the direction avoided by Miss Winter. Then he turned and looked at his interlocutress as if to enjoy the triumph of having baffled her. For a moment she was conscious of a subtle humiliation—she felt as if she were forming part of a victor's triumphal procession. The next instant she smiled into his eyes. A woman rather likes the degradation of being overcome by a man ; it keeps up her healthy respect for the sex—a respect which few of us cultivate with conspicuous success.

"As I was telling Miss Grace before lunch," continued Tyars, before the pause grew irksome, " you will not see this old ship again."

" So Oswin told me. You both speak of it in a very heartless way. I always understood that sailors were so devoted to their ships."

"Seems," said Oswin, "rather like hiring a man to save your life, and dismissing him with a shilling extra and a smile when he has done it."

"We could not bring the ship back so far from sentimental motives," said Tyars, in a matter-of-fact way; and he spoke with that hardness which is only found in certain ranges of society, and strange to say, one finds it in the same social altitude in France as in England. Its chief characteristic is negative, for it conveys a subtle and yet flat refusal to admit that there is anything in life worth getting flurried about. It will not recognize the existence of any emotion which cannot be lived down. And yet these people, educated descendants of educated men and women, are just those who know how to suffer most. Education and

hereditary refinement are the seed and hot-
bed of that sensibility to which pain can be
most cruel. This is no doubt only another
illustration of that serene adaptability to
circumstances which characterizes the work-
ings of Nature in everything. If the body
can adapt itself, if one eye can assume the
responsibility of two, if one lung can do its
fellow's work in addition to its own, why
should not the heart learn to adapt itself to
new emotions ? For new emotions must be
provided ; is there not a quill-wielding army
seeking daily for them ? And these new
emotions bring new antidotes. There are
many cures as there are many maladies of
the heart—the ridicule cure, the cynicism
cure, the novelty cure, the excitement cure,
but surest of all the living-down. As in
physical diseases there are certain tough
hearts to which only the strongest anticor
can penetrate, and for these the living-down

cure is alone effectual. Claud Tyars was just the man to adopt at once and with forethought the most stringent measures. In this he only followed the instincts of the class of which he was an unusually perfect specimen—the hard-limbed product of English public school and university. If one takes a square inch of bone from the leg of a thorough-bred horse and place it in comparison with the same portion taken from the limb of a dray-horse, the magic touch of breed and blood can be detected at once. The thorough-bred bone is hard and close and white like ivory; the other is gray and porous. So is it with human hearts—that of the man or woman descended from refined and educated ancestors is purer and whiter and more delicate; but it is also harder. Claud Tyars was no doubt a hard-hearted man, else he would not have slipped so readily into the post of command which seemed to be waiting for him. He had a strong belief in the subservience of the emotions to convenience. He was the very antitype to those individuals who fall in love with barmaids or run amuck among the prejudices of their relatives. And so, after all, he assisted Miss Winter and Matthew Mark Easton beyond their expectation. Presently he left the group, for he had other duties to attend to, although the pilot was in charge. There was no confusion, no shouting on board this little ship, but all went smoothly with that mixed discipline of the yacht and the man-of-war which Easton had commented upon.

The moments dwindled on with the slow, dragging monotony which characterizes latest moments, and makes us almost impatient to see the last of faces which we shall perhaps never look upon again.

Presently the town of Gravesend hove in sight, and all on the quarter-deck of the *Argo* gazed at it as they might have gazed on some unknown Eastern city after traversing the desert. And then after all—all the waiting, the preparation, the counting of moments, and the calculating of distances— the bell in the engine-room came as a surprise. There was something startling in the clang of the gong as the engineer replied.

Helen was the last to rise. She stood holding the shawl which Oswin had spread over her knees, and looked round with a strange intense gaze. There are moments when the human brain becomes sensitized like a photographer's dry-plate, and the impressions received during those moments are clear, distinct, and imperishable like a finished photograph.

The steamer was now drifting slowly on the tide with resting engines. There were two boats rowing towards her from Gravesend Pier, one a low, green-painted wherry for the pilot, the other a larger boat with stained and faded red cushions. The scene —the torpid yellow river, the sordid town and low riverside warehouses—could scarce have been exceeded for pure unvarnished dismalness.

Already the steps were being lowered. In a few moments the larger boat swung alongside, held by a rope made fast in the forecastle of the *Argo*. A general move was made towards the rail. Tyars passed out on to the gangway, where he stood waiting to hand the ladies into the boat. Helen was near to her brother; she turned to him and kissed him in silence. Then she went to the gangway. There was a little pause, and for a moment Helen and Tyars were left alone at the foot of the brass-bound steps.

"Good-bye," said Tyars.

There was a slight prolongation of the last syllable as if he had something else to say; but he never said it, although she gave him time.

"Good-bye," she answered at length, and she too seemed to have something to add which was never added.

Then she stepped lightly into the boat and took her place on the faded red cushions.

The *Argo* went to sea that night. There was much to do, although everything seemed to be in its place, and every man appeared to know his duty. It thus happened that Tyars and Grace had not a moment to themselves until well on into the night. The watch was set at eight o'clock. For a moment Tyars paused before leaving his chief officer alone on the little bridge.

" What a clever fellow Easton is ! " he said. " I never recognized it until this afternoon."

" Um-m," returned Oswin Grace, without lowering his glasses.

CHAPTER X.

A HORRIBLE TASK.

THERE are many people who go through life without ever knowing what it is to fight a gale of wind. Dwellers in cities know indeed that the wild winds blow when they hear the hum of strained wires overhead, when the dust rises in whirls at every street corner, when the sanitary *employés* have difficulty in capturing small truant paper-bags that refuse to recognize their cart or power, and when it is really inconvenient to wear high hats and light-minded skirts.

Those who live at the edge of the sea will never admit that they know little about a gale of wind, when at equinoctial periods their windows require cleaning every day, when face and hair are sticky with salt rime, and there is a pleasant sharpness of taste on either lip. Their gale is a matter of staying indoors, of avoiding the sea-wall, and carefully closing all windows. The sea is yellow and disturbed; far away it is of a peculiar light green, like dead pea-pods, and from its bosom there arises a thin white veil of spray, and there is no perspective. Sky and water meet in a gray uncertainty a short way beyond the pier-head. Occasionally a dripping coaster, some close-reefed brig mayhap, or a tiny schooner moves across the near horizon, making better weather of it than one would think.

Sailors of course have the monopoly of wind and weather. They alone are

competent to judge whether it be a whole
gale or half, or a mere capful of wind. It is
their trade and calling to tussle with the
elements.   And Boreas is their chiefest
enemy ; without the double warmth of oil-
skins and hope I think there would be very
few sailors.

This preliminary leads where most thin
and watery pathways do, into a gale of
wind, and such a gale as few mortals ever
have to meet. The tropics are gifted in this
way ; there have you cyclones, typhoons,
tornados, aracans, vuthans, white squalls
and black squalls, north-easters, monsoons,
and the wild changes thereof. Of these
most of us must perforce judge from the
standpoint of our own paltry breezes, our
bises, our siroccos and thin south-westers,
our mistrals and Danubian squalls. All
these long-named winds are cruel, but kill-
ing is not their mission. There is, how-

ever, a breath of heaven of which the sole
message is death. It is a wind with no
fine-sounding name, for it belongs to the
North, where men endure things and have
no thought of naming them. It blows for
six months of the year, with here and there
a breathing space wherein to gather fresh
impetuosity. It veers from south-south-west
to north-west-by-north, and it is born upon
the gray ice-fields round the pole. For many
hundred miles it raves across the frozen
ocean, gathering deathly coldness at every
league. On its shoulders it carries tons of
snow, and then striking land it rages and
tears, howls, moans, and screams across
Northern Europe into far-frozen Asia. In
passing it clothes all Russia in white and
still has plenty to spare for bleak Siberia,
Northern China, and Japan. I have crouched
and shivered beneath its breath, and the
only thought that was not frozen up was

that the prevalence of such a wind must assuredly depopulate any land. As a matter of fact this is almost the case, although a few northern races manage to live on in such numbers as to save extermination, and that is all. More than a third of them are partially or wholly blind. Their existence is a constant and unequal struggle against this same wind and its pitiless auxiliaries— snow and frost. The earth yields no increase here. A little sparse vegetation, sufficient only to nourish miserable reindeer and a few horses; a scattering of pine-trees, and that is all. Although no sanctifying Spirit can be said to walk upon the waters, the sea alone sustains life, for men, dogs, and reindeer eat fish, not dried but frozen, when they can get it.

It was across this country, and in face of this wind, that a party of men and women made their way in the late summer five years ago. By late summer one means the first fortnight in July in these high latitudes. These travellers were twenty-one in number, sixteen men and five women. One woman carried a baby—a gaol-bird—born in prison—unbaptized. It did not count, not even as half a person, to any one except its mother. Men and women were dressed alike in good fur clothing, baggy trousers tucked into felt boots, long blouse-like fur coats, and caps with ear-flaps tied down. Boots, trousers, coats, and even caps bore signs of damage by water. When Northern Siberia is not frozen up it is in a state of flood, and travelling, except by water, is almost impossible. These people had come many miles by this comparatively easy method at imminent risk, for they had travelled north on the bosom of the flood. Since then they had literally burnt their vessels in order to cut off pursuit.

The men dragged light sledges, three to a sledge, and four resting. The women carried various more precious burdens, delicate instruments such as compasses and aneroids. Beneath the fur caps throbbed some singular brains, from under the draggled brims looked out some strange faces. There was a doctor among them, two army officers, a judge, and others who had not been allowed time to become anything, for they were exiled while students.

The whole party pressed forward in silence with tight-locked lips and half-closed eyes, for the rushing wind carried a fine blinding snow before it. Only one person spoke at times. It was the woman who carried the baby, and she interlarded her inconsequent remarks with snatches of song and bursts of peculiar cackling laughter. Suddenly she sat down on a boulder.

"I will sit here," she said, "in the warm sun."

The whole party stopped, and one of the women answered—

"Come, Anna," she said, "we cannot wait here." Still speaking she took her arm and urged her to rise.

"But," protested she who had been addressed as Anna, "where is the picnic to be?"

"The picnic, Anna Pavloski," said a small, squarely-built man, coming forward and speaking in a wonderfully deep and harmonious tone of voice, "is to be held farther on. You must come at once."

"I think," she replied, gently, "that I will wait here for my husband. I expect him home from the office. He will bring the newspaper."

They were all grouped round the woman now except one man, and he stood apart

with his back turned towards them.   He
had been dragging the foremost sledge, and
the broad band of the trace was still across
his shoulders.   He had been leading the
way, and seemed in some subtle manner to
be recognized as chief and pioneer.

Again the woman who had first spoken
persuaded ; again the broad-shouldered man
spoke in his commanding gentleness.   It
was, however, of no avail.   Then after a
few moments of painful hesitation, he left
the group and went to where the leader
stood alone.

" Pavloski," he said.

" Yes, doctor."   He never turned his head,
but stood, rigid and stern, looking straight
before him, scowling with eyes from which
the horror would now never fade, into the
gray hopeless distance.   No marble statue
could reproduce the strong cold despair that
breathed in every limb and feature.

"Something," said the doctor, "must be done. We are behind our time already."

"I suppose it is my duty to stay with you?" said Pavloski; "I cannot leave the party? I cannot stay behind?"

The little man made no answer. His silence was more eloquent than any words could have been. A dramatic painter could scarcely have found a sadder picture than these two friends who dared not to meet each other's eyes. And yet, in a moment, it was rendered infinitely sadder by the advent of a third person.

Swathed as she was in furs, it was difficult to distinguish that this was a woman at all, and yet to a close observer her movements, the manner in which she set her feet upon the ground, the suggestion of graceful curves in limb and form, betrayed that she was indeed a young girl. Her face confirmed it—gay blue eyes and a rosebud mouth, round cheeks delicately tinted despite the wild wind, and little wisps of golden hair straggling out beneath the ear-flaps, and gleaming against the dusky face.

" I," said this little woman, " will stay with her. Sergius, I will try and take her back. We will give ourselves up. It does not matter. Now that Hans is dead I have nothing to live for. I have no husband."

Poor little maiden, she had never had a husband; the fatherly Russian Government had seen to that! But she chose to call Hans Onetcheff her husband. This same Onetcheff had been administratively exiled by mistake, and being delicate had died, at the mines, of prison consumption.

The little doctor winced. He was not a Nihilist at all, and never had been ; but in personal appearance he had resembled one. There was something horribly real in the words that came from the girl's rosy lips.

She shouted them, for the wind was so furious as to render conversation impossible ; and in order to make herself heard, she raised her round cherub-like face with a very fascinating childishness of manner. Sergius Pavloski shook his head and moved a step or two towards the group half hidden by a fine driving snow.

"No," he answered. "We arranged it before leaving London. There is only one thing to be done."

The doctor and the girl exchanged a look of horror, and hesitated to follow him.

"It was agreed," he continued, mechanically, "that the lives of all were never to be endangered for the sake of one. Tyars said that."

Slowly the two followed him. As they approached the group some of these stepped silently back, some walked away a few paces and stood apart with averted faces.

"Can you tell me," said the woman, looking up suddenly, and leaving the baby's face and throat fully exposed to the cruel wind, "whether I can find a lodging near here?"

She addressed Pavloski, who was standing in front of her. He made no answer, but presently turned away with a convulsive movement of lips and throat, as if he were swallowing something with an effort. Then he raised his voice, and addressing his companions generally, he said with the assurance of a man placed in a position to exact obedience—

"Will you all go on? Keep the same direction, north-by-west according to the compass. I shall catch you up before evening."

He stood quite still, like a man hewn out of stone—upright, emotionless, and quite determined—awaiting the fulfilment of his commands. All around him his companions waited. It almost seemed as if they expected the Almighty to interfere. Even to those who have tasted the bitterest cup that life has ever brewed, this seemed too cruel to be true—too horrid! And the wind blew all around them, tearing, raging on. Some of them staggered a little, but none made a movement to obey the command of their leader; each seemed to dread setting an example to the others.

At last one man had the courage to do it. It was he who had spoken to Pavloski, the man whom they called doctor. He went towards one of the sledges and proceeded to disentangle the traces thrown carelessly down when a halt had been called. The men stepped silently forward and drew the cords across their shoulders.

The women moved away first, stepping softly on the silent snow, and like phantoms vanishing in the mist and windy turmoil. The men followed, dragging their noiseless sledges. The doctor stayed behind for a moment. When the others were out of earshot he went towards Pavloski and laid his mittened hand upon his arm.

"Sergius," he said with painful hesitation, "let me do it—I am a doctor—it will be easier."

Pavloski turned and looked at the speaker in a stupid, bewildered way, as if the language used were unknown to him. Then he smiled suddenly in a sickening way; it was like a cynical smile upon the face of the dead.

"Go!" he said, pointing to windward, where their companions had disappeared. "Go with them. Let each one of us do his duty. It will be a consolation whatever the end may be."

The doctor was bound in honour to obey

this man in all and through all. He obeyed now, and left Sergius Pavloski alone with his mad wife and his helpless babe. As he moved away he heard the woman prattling of the sun, and the birds, and the flowers.

He turned his face resolutely northwards and pressed forward into the icy wind; but a muffled gurgling shriek broke down his strong resolution. Without stopping, he glanced back over his shoulder with a gasp of horror. Sergius Pavloski was kneeling with his back to the north; but he was not kneeling on the snow, for the doctor saw two fur-clad arms waving convulsively, and between the soles of Pavloski's great snow-boots he caught sight of two other feet drawn up in agony.

"Good God," exclaimed the man aloud, "forgive him!"

And with bloodshot eyes and haggard lips he stumbled on, not heeding where he set his feet. He fell, and rose again, scarce knowing what he did. Despite the freezing wind, the perspiration ran down his face, blinding him. It froze, and hung in little icicles on his moustache and beard.

"Good God," he mumbled again, "forgive him!"

And in the agony of his strong mind his brain lost all power of concentration. His lips continued to frame those four words over and over and over again, until they became bereft of all meaning, and lapsed into a mere rhythmic refrain, keeping time with the swing of his sturdy legs.

CHAPTER XI.

IT is a thousand pities that Englishmen, Americans, Russians, Scandinavians, and others of a Northern nationality are so difficult to write about. The manner in which these large men persistently ignore the emotions, and continuously refuse to play to the gallery, as it were, simply forces the astute novelist to seek material elsewhere. And so we have the Anglo-Italian, the Anglo-French, the Anglo-South American novel. They are so picturesque, these Giovannis, and Pippis, and Andrés. They bubble over so conveniently with love rhapsodies; they are so deft with their knives; and their *per bacchos* and *sacrés* and *carrambas* look so well in italics— lending a local colour, you know. And then it is so easy to know what they are about because they are so frankly emotional. They weep so often, and usually on the bosom of an aged mother, or beneath the shadow of the " Porto del Popolo," or some other porto that sounds local in its tendency ; while an honest English young man called John or Andrew never gives one a chance. One cannot make obvious to the gallery the emotions that are passing within his breast because he absolutely refuses to gesticulate, to cast himself about upon the furniture, or to apostrophize the heavens. And the greater portion of English-speaking novel readers is, so to speak, the gallery.

There is small consolation to be derived

from that self-complacency born of a con-
viction that virtue is sometimes unre-
warded. The little boy who tells the truth
generally has a bad time, while the small
follower of Ananias walks in the sunshine
of popularity. We do not generally admit
this unfortunate fact in mixed circles on
account of the children, but it is there
nevertheless. And the children grow up—
some of them alas! grow up into novelists,
others into felons. The seed is sown in
the one as in the other, and neither seem
capable of helping it. It is with the novelists that we have to do. Young Ananias
possesses an imagination, and he proceeds
to tell most iniquitous . . . No! I mean
he goes on to describe men and women,
who not only have never lived, but to
whom life would be impossible in this
matter-of-fact planet. He draws lurid pic-
tures of adventure in countries which he

has only seen casually on the map—he describes deeds of bravery and feats of agility which any common-sense person must recognize at once as quite impossible. Perhaps he has a far-reaching, an unclean mind ; he proceeds to wallow in realistic details which are not only sickening, but totally untrue to nature. Never mind ! Ananias gets on famously, comes out in weekly parts in the cheap newspapers, and finishes up in a yellow-back novel on the railway book-stalls depicting the murder of one faultlessly dressed gentleman by another — an every - day occurrence, of course.

Now the unpopular good boy drones away his time in descriptions of events that really happen or have happened. He sets down men and women as he has seen and known them, he narrates their deeds in such language as he commands, and neglects to conjure up impossibilities for them to perpetrate. He sacrifices dramatic construction on the altar of Truth, and fails to make use of certain well-known devices. He does not, for instance, cause a son to narrate at length to the mother whose skirt he has never left the sad story of his own life in the first volume. He does not make husband and wife exchange terrible confidences after twelve or thirteen years of married life—said confidences being of such a nature that unless they had habited different parts of the globe mutual concealment would have been quite impossible. No; this blind fictionist makes his fiction possible ; he tells the truth, and of course he is unpopular.

If Matthew Mark Easton had arrived in St. Petersburg in any other manner it should have been narrated here. If he had come down in the middle of the Admiralty gardens in a Nihilistic balloon in the dead of night the details of his descent should have been set down here. If he had exchanged mysterious meaningless paraphrases with picturesque conspirators those observations should have been faithfully given here—in italics. But he did none of these things. He merely arrived by train from Libau, and took a droschky to the Hôtel de France for which he paid seventy kopecks. His passport was in perfect order, although smeared most lamentably by the clerk of the Russian consulate who *viséd* it in London. This small American was an experienced and clever traveller, as most of his countrymen are, and was as much at home in St. Petersburg as he might have been in Boston or London. Moreover, he had been in St. Petersburg and in the Hôtel de France before. His nationality was also in those days fraught with a certain weight of favourable prejudice, for that was three years ago, before the Siberian question had attracted transatlantic attention.

Matthew Mark Easton therefore made himself quite at home in the Hôtel de France, and dined very comfortably at the *table d'hôte*, of which certain small eccentricities failed to surprise him. He lighted his interprandial cigarette at the candle placed between each two guests for the purpose, and fell very naturally into Slavonic habits; but it is perhaps worth noticing that he somewhat carefully concealed his knowledge of the Russian language. This alone was proof of his intimacy with the internal economy of the White Empire; for old travellers there know that it is better to reserve one's Russian for a necessity, even if he have no other purpose than enjoyment in his wanderings. After dinner he retired to his room, not however without being forced to ward off several singularly leading questions put to him by a bland landlord. These questions were obviously of one and the same purpose; namely, to discover the reason of Easton's presence in Russia. Had he been there before? Did he admire the town? Was not the Newski Prospect unrivalled? Where was he going after he quitted the Northern capital? To all of these Matthew Mark Easton replied vaguely and almost densely, with a singularly strong American accent. He was not surprised to be awakened the next morning by the wildest carillon that ever pealed from cathedral spire, for he had heard the remarkable performance of St. Michael's bells before.

After breakfast he wandered forth, guide-book in hand, having refused the services of a polyglot individual who professed to be the brother-in-law of the hall-porter. The landlord himself directed Easton to the

Newski Prospect, which however was not considered interesting until the afternoon. Nevertheless he went that way, and finally found himself on the English quay. He crossed the Neva, still in the same tourist's gait, and lost himself among the smaller commercial streets of the Vasili Ostroff. Presently by the merest accident he found himself opposite a small warehouse bearing the name " L. Ogroff" in painted letters above the blind windows of what had once been a shop. He pushed open the curtained door, and addressing himself to a pleasant-looking girl who was seated at a counter adding up the columns of a ledger, he mentioned the name "Loris Ogroff."

" Yes," answered the girl in perfect English, " he is in. Who are you ? "

" Matthew Mark Easton."

" Ah ! Come in."

She pointed to a little swing-door in the

counter, and did not offer to open it as a born and bred servitor would have done. Then she led the way into an inner room which was lined with shelves containing long wooden boxes like miniature coffins. There were upon the table some rolls of common cloth.

"Mr. Ogroff is apparently a tailor," hazarded Easton in a conversational way, seeing that the girl was pretty and pleasant-looking.

"Yes," she answered, with a short laugh; "a very cheap one."

She had not relinquished her hold of the door-handle, and stood in a graceful attitude looking at him with clear blue eyes, in which a great interest and a slight amusement were provokingly mingled. She evidently knew all about him, and her attitude physical and mental was notably devoid of that shyness or embarrassment which is considered correct and polite between young persons of opposite sexes who meet without introduction.

" He is up-stairs in the cutting-out room," she continued, with a twinkle in her childish eyes. " I shall tell him."

Easton stood looking at the curtained door after she had closed it. Then he picked up a piece of rough cloth and examined its texture critically.

" I am half inclined," he reflected aloud, " to become a Nihilist. There are alleviations even in the lot of a tailor's assistant of the establishment Ogroff."

In a few moments the door opened again, and a stout man entered with a bow. He shook hands without speaking, and pointed to a chair. Round his thick neck he wore a yellow tape-measure with the two ends hanging down in front. Before speaking he took up some rolls of cloth that stood in the corner, and unfolding a portion of each he ranged them upon the table in front of Easton.

We last saw this man in Easton's rooms in London. His name was not mentioned then because there was not much in a name for him. It was not Ogroff then. He was not minutely described, because a written description is not always of great value. For instance, he was in London a dark grizzled man with a beard—in this shop in the Vasili Ostroff, St. Petersburg, he was a fair, hairless man.

" Well ? " he said asthmatically at length.

" Not a word . . . ! " replied Easton ; " and you ? "

The man shrugged his heavy shoulders.

" Not a word. I have written to you all that I heard. I wrote on the fifth of May ; have you destroyed the letter ? "

" Yes—burnt it."

" Well ! " ejaculated the Russian, misusing the word. " I heard," he continued,—"never mind how—that they all got away, in good health, at the proper time—that is, in the early summer of the year before last. They were followed, but they destroyed all the horses and boats as they went, and the pursuit was necessarily given up."

" Since that," inquired Easton, " not a word ? "

" Not·a word."

" There has been no semi-official account of the matter in the newspapers ? "

" No ; it has been hushed up. The official report is (as far as I can learn) that certain exiles and prisoners escaped ; that they were pursued by Cossacks, and that the chase was only given up when their death by starvation was a moral certainty."

" And," said Easton, " are they struck out of the list ? "

" Yes ; they are struck out."

The fat man spoke in a gasping way, and his breathing was attended by a peculiar hollow sound. It was noticeable that he never paused to think before replying to any question, and never referred to note-book or written memorandum. All his information was on the surface ready for use, and all his memoranda were mental. One cannot search in a man's mind for in-criminating evidence. He who at present passed under the name of Loris Ogroff was known among his colleagues as an eminently " safe " man.

" I am going to look for them," announced Easton, after a pause.

The Russian raised his flaxen eyebrows.

" Ah ! I understood that you were con-demned—by the doctors."

" No, not condemned ; they merely said, ' If you go it will kill you.' "

"And still," said the Russian, calmly, "you go."

"Some one must," answered Easton with equal coolness. "You cannot—you are too fat!"

"No; I do not travel now as I used. Besides, I have other work. My hands are full, as well as my waistcoat."

"I am going by land," continued the American. "I leave Petersburg to-morrow morning."

Ogroff rose from his chair.

"You must go now," he said. "You have been here long enough; we are watched, you know. Here in Petersburg we all watch each other. I will send you a fur-lined travelling cloak to-night to your hotel —the Hôtel de France, I suppose?"

"Yes; how do you know?"

"I get a copy of each day's passport-returns from a friend of mine in the police."

"But," protested Easton, "I do not want a fur cloak."

"Never matter; it will be useful—you can give it away.   It is to allay suspicion."

"All right; send it."

The Russian held out a fat white hand.

"Good-bye, you brave American," he said.

"G'bye!" returned Easton with a laugh.

CHAPTER XII.

THEY TRIED IT.

"WELL, at all events we have tried it!"
Ordinary words if it please you! Ordinary words enough in all sooth, and words we must all make use of sooner or later. But all words are ordinary, and it is only the manner of speaking them, the circumstances in which they are spoken, and the person to hear, that lend a human interest to the tritest commonplaces.

These words were spoken by the mere remnant of a man to a solitary companion while both looked out—peered through the twilight—on death. He who spoke crouched in a singular way on the hard snow, supporting himself on one fur-clad arm. He could not stand, for he had but one leg. The other had been cut off just above the knee—a recent amputation undoubtedly, for the empty trouser-leg, rudely tied with rope, was stained a deep suggestive colour. His face was a horrid sight to look upon, for here and there in the pasty yellow flesh were deep indentations of half-healed sores, the result of frost-bite. One eye was quite closed by a swelling which deformed the features and drew them all up. He spoke in a mumbling way, as if his tongue were swollen or diseased, and the language was the most dramatic of all tongues—Russian.

His companion, a short, thick-set man, stood beside him; but he stood weakly, and the terribly sunken lines of his cheeks told a story only slightly less horrible than that

depicted by the face and form of the cripple.
Both faces alike bore that strange dry look
which tells unerringly of starvation. All
who were in Southern India at the time
of the Madras famine know that look, and
those who have never seen it before divine
its meaning at once. It is unmistakable,
like an earthquake.

Behind these two men lay a vast snow-
clad country, rolling away in rounded gray
curves into fathomless mist. On their left
was a slight declivity, terminated by a broad
flat valley, extending beyond sight in a due
southerly direction. This was the river
Yana. Within a few yards of the two men,
at their backs, stood a rude, ill-shapen hut,
built clumsily and ignorantly of snow. Its
low doorway faced the north, and amidst
the gloom of its interior there were dis-
cernible a number of heaps, apparently
formed of old and tattered fur clothing.

These were dead men; the women of Sergius Pavloski's party had not lived to see the Arctic Ocean. Amidst the dead the living had crouched and slept that dull, dreamless sleep that comes to human beings in extremely cold climates. In front of the two men extended that which had been their bourne, their hope, their one desire— the Arctic Ocean. There was no water visible, but as far as the eye could penetrate a heaving, surging field of pack-ice. Low down in the far northern sky there hovered a yellow shimmer—the ice-blink.

It was the second of September, and in all probability the ice was gathering for the winter. Already it extended along the deserted shore, in a belt twenty miles deep, without a lead, and from the continuous sounds of groaning and grinding it was certain that more was pressing in, adding confusion to the frozen chaos. The man who stood gave a short heartrending laugh as he looked out over the frozen sea.

" Yes," he said, " we have tried it."

There was a pause, and then the cripple —Sergius Pavloski—spoke again.

" Of course," he said, almost unintelligibly, "we have failed ; but still our failure may teach others, and we have kept it secret. Those who want to know will never know. They will always be in uncertainty as to whether we have escaped and are living hidden in America, in Europe, perhaps in Russia. We shall be more terrible, doctor, dead than alive."

" I hope so."

" I, at all events, shall be, for you say that I could not live a week in a warm climate. This leg of mine is less painful to-day ; perhaps it is healing."

" No, Pavloski, I have told you a dozen times it is not healed, it is only frozen. It can never heal. The moment it thaws you will die."

A sickly smile passed across his unsightly features, and there was silence for a time— the deathly expectant silence of the far North. They were both looking out across the ice. It was a habit they had acquired during the last two months. At length Pavloski raised his mittened hand and extended it outwards true north, like the needle of a compass.

" I wonder," he mumbled, " if Tyars is out there."

The doctor shrugged his broad shoulders.

" I wonder," he said, " why you entrusted this to an Englishman."

It was an old subject thoroughly thrashed out; an old point of dissension. When men see death staring them in the face they are not conversational on general topics; they only discuss their chances of life.

"If I had had the whole world to choose from I should not have selected another man," said Pavloski; "but there was no choice in the matter."

"I suppose," said the doctor, with an ill-concealed sneer, "that he has turned back."

"I will swear by St. Paul that he has not done that!"

The words were not pleasant to hear from lips already stiffening in anticipation of death.

"Then where is he?"

"Dead!" was the answer. "If Claud Tyars had been alive he would have come. He is not here, therefore he is dead!— Ough!"

He stopped and fell back fainting with pain. In his excitement he had moved, and had allowed some of his weight to rest upon the raw stump of his leg. In a second the doctor was kneeling on the snow beside him, raising his head, touching his lips with snow. It was a poor restorative, but there was nothing else at hand. One cannot offer to a dying man even the tenderest piece of an old sealskin mitten.

Without waiting for consciousness to return he attempted to lift the cripple, intending to carry him within the little snow-hut, but the movement brought back Pavloski's failing senses, and he shook his head in token that he wished to be left where he lay.

" No," he said, after gasping twice for breath ; " I would rather die out here."

The doctor's bare hand crept within the tattered sleeve towards the pulse. He said nothing. There was nothing to say.

" I do not want," continued Pavloski, brokenly, " to see their—faces. I—brought them here.—It is my fault."

He lay for some moments with his lips apart, his uninjured eye half closed, then he spoke again.

"I suppose—the good God—will know how to revenge all this.—If they, the Romanoffs—the Czar—had twenty lives, and we could take—them all—we might pay—the debt;—but they have—only one life—to take, that would be too short—a punishment. God will know how to do it —will He not, doctor?"

"Yes," said the sweet deep voice of the doctor, "God will know how to do t."

"Pray," said the dying man, "pray to Him to do it—well!"

Then his head fell back and he breathed regularly and softly. But this was not the end. Presently the blackened lips began to move, and he spoke in quite a different voice, so different as to startle his listener.

It was soft and even, as if recounting a dream not long dispelled.

"It is not yet a year ago," he said. "There were seven of us, four Russians, two Englishmen, and an American. Four Russians, two Englishmen, and an American—what a strong combination! The Russians to go into action on land, the Englishmen on the sea, and the sharp-witted American to watch and plot and scheme. I remember the last time we met was at Easton's house; we eat and drank together. Two of us are dead, and I am nearly—dead. Tyars and Grace—where can they be? They are out there, doctor, in front of us— to the north. I—I shall go and . . . meet them."

The lips closed with a sudden snap, and the doctor leant eagerly forward. Sergius Pavloski was dead. Perhaps his babbled words were true. He said that he would go to meet them, and it is not for us to maintain that this was the mere wandering of a mind harassed by much affliction, paralyzed by the cold touch of Death. It is not for us to assert that the departing soul is never vouchsafed a gleam of light, of that Light which is not seen on land or sea, to guide it upward to its rest. Perhaps indeed he had gone to meet them, to find these two Englishmen in whom his faith had never wavered.

Then the survivor rose to his feet. It had begun to snow gently and in large flakes—a snow that would cover the ground to the depth of twelve inches in half that number of hours. As it fell it gradually covered the dead man, even to his face and eyes, which were already cold.

Presently the doctor moved a little and, turning slowly round, scanned the near horizon. He could not see the pack-ice now, for the snow was blowing in from the north, wreathing and curling as it came. The wind had dropped a little, and so the ice was still, and its groan was heard no more. The silence was terrible—that silence that comes between two squalls at sea. Suddenly the snow ceased, and only a few feathery flakes floated aimlessly in the air. The atmosphere cleared and displayed to the man's dim vision a lifeless world of virgin white. Even the footsteps of his late companion and himself were half obliterated; the body of Sergius Pavloski was covered, and presented the appearance of a churchyard mound, for the snow had drifted heavily at the first rush of the squall.

Then this lone man moved towards the snow-hut, and entered it on his hands and knees. He took no notice of the dead— one soon gets accustomed to them—but fumbled about among the baggage piled up in one corner.

While he worked he mumbled to himself. Probably he was only half conscious of his actions, as men are in extreme cold. It is very easy to sit in a warm room and reflect that we should never lose our heads in a snowstorm; that we should never be so weak-minded as to give way to that dazed drowsiness which comes from snow alone. Fatigues on land or sea have their characteristics, but in neither case is the brain affected as it is by a great fatigue borne on snow. Mountaineers know this, and the good brothers of St. Bernard; they know that the strongest man is forced to use his utmost strength of mind to keep serene and calm while battling on snow against a snowstorm; whereas an ordinary sailor-man, of no great courage, can face a gale almost unmoved.

But this man's bodily strength seemed
to be almost unimpaired. He dragged the
heavy sledges aside without any great effort.
He had been, and was still, a man of
exceptional strength—broadly built upon
short legs, with a large square head. It
was somewhat singular that he should be
apparently far from death while his companions had succumbed to cold and starvation; but this undoubtedly lay in the fact
that he was a doctor. His intimate knowledge of the human frame had doubtless
enabled him to take a greater care of himself than he could force upon his companions. He had, no doubt, been strong
enough in purpose to endure a hunger
which his dead comrades had satisfied by
illegitimate means. This is no place to go
into details, for these pages may come to
the eyes of many who will be no wiser
and no better for learning aught of death.

Indeed, it is difficult to imagine that any of us are in any way benefited by a study of this subject from a fictional point of view. We meet it often enough in real life.

That strange law which we call Chance has one singular trick; it almost invariably sets the wrong man in the wrong place. This is, of course, according to the limit of our terrestrial sight, as the Scotch ministers so frequently say; though it would be hard for us to see with any other sight, so the rider is superfluous. This Russian doctor was an instance of the perverseness of Chance. He was not a Nihilist, though he had been mistaken for one, which, as far as he was concerned, came to the same thing. He was not made of that stuff out of which are fashioned lonely adventurers, solitary travellers, or self-sufficing Stoics. He was merely a garrulous, gregarious little fellow with a decided bodily tendency to stoutness, which tendency had not been fairly treated. He had never lived alone— had never thought of doing such a thing. What a man, you will say, to place upon the edge of the frozen Arctic Ocean with no human life within a radius of three hundred miles, in the month of September! Exactly so. But that is precisely the man whom Chance would select to place there. More- over she made that selection—hence this record. From among those iron-hearted, desperate fugitives, she carefully chose the wrong man to be last survivor; for there is no such thing as the Survival of the Fittest, though we write it with the capital- est of letters. Chance sees to that.

And yet in a dull, stupid way he realized the responsibilities of his position. He dragged two of the sledges out of the hut, and with a hatchet broke them up. Then he took the two strongest pieces of each—

the crossbars—and bound them securely together, thus forming a rough pole. This he erected on a little mound where the snow was thin, building it up with such debris as he could lay his hands upon. It stood up gauntly, almost the only object within sight that was not white. It was a mere pole, the thickness of a man's wrist, and yet it was probably visible ten miles off against its gleaming surroundings.

When this was completed there was nothing left for him to do. There was no record to be preserved—no record of the sufferings and of the great struggle. The earlier acts of the tragedy were lost, and no earthly lips left to tell of them. After all, what did it matter? The last act wiped them all out. When the game is played there is nothing to be gained by the recapitulation of its chances.

The lone man stood back and contemplated his rude erection. It was rough, but strong enough to last a year or two. Then he looked at the remains of the light American sledges which he had just broken up.

Suddenly an idea came to him.

" It would be good," he mumbled, " to be warm once more . . . just once."

And he piled up the wood in a little heap. He crawled into the hut and presently returned bearing a good-sized tin bottle labelled " Spiritus." He poured the contents over the wood and struck a match. In a moment the blue flames leapt up and the wood crackled. He crouched down to the leeward side so close that his clothes were singed and gave forth a sharp acrid smell. He withdrew his mittens and held his bare scarred hands right into the flames.

"Ah," he muttered in a gurgling voice, " that is good !"

But it did not last long. The wood was light and very dry, and in five minutes there was nothing left but a few smouldering ashes.

The doctor rose to his feet and looked long and steadily out to the north over the broken ice. It is hard to give up hope, and few men are ever forced to do so. Then he looked round him as a man looks round a room before starting on a long journey to see that he has left nothing undone. He had lived in this spot for more than two months, and its bleak surroundings were very familiar to him. His eyes lingered over each white mound and hillock—not lovingly, for it was horribly dismal, almost too dismal to be part of this world at all.

Strange to say his eyes finished their inspection by looking up to heaven. The great snow-clouds were rolling south, bearing in their huge rounded bosoms the white pall to cover a continent for many months to come. But this man seemed to be looking beyond the clouds, seeking to penetrate the dim ether. He was not looking at the sky, but into heaven. At last he gave a contemptuous little shrug of the shoulders, full of a terrible meaning. The next moment he sought for something in the inner pocket of his fur tunic. There was a gleam of dull rusted metal, and he raised his hand towards his open mouth. At the same instant a sharp report broke upon that echoless silence, and a little puff of white smoke was borne southward on the breeze.

CHAPTER XIII.

THREE YEARS AFTER.

THERE are some women to whom even
Time is merciful. It is an undeniable
truth that those among our gentle companions through this pilgrimage who are fair
to look upon may surely count upon some
allowance from men both young and old.
Charity may cover a multitude of sins—
perhaps it does ; I cannot say, for I have
never had an opportunity of studying its
habits for any length of time. But Beauty
undoubtedly covers more. Not only have
plain women to bear with a thousand
minute slights from every pretty face they

meet, but if they be observant they will realize soon enough that there is a special code of laws tacitly allowed to the owners of these pretty faces. They have no need to be scrupulous; it does not matter much that they be honest, so long as they are gracious, and fascinating, and kind at intervals. The necessity of working for their own livelihood is rarely forced upon them. Beauty in distress is proverbially sure of relief. But there is one enemy upon whom all charms are lost, to whose heart red lips, soft hands, and pleading eyes cannot reach. This enemy is Time. It is not only around dull eyes that he scores his mark; he touches rosy cheeks and pale alike; he sets his weight upon straight shoulders as on crooked bones. But some there are to whom he is kind, and these are usually such as fear him not. Some folks are said to defy Time, but it is safer to meet him with a fearless smile,

for he is not to be defied. He carries more
in his hands than we can tell or dare defy.
Agnes Winter was not the woman to make
this mistake, and Time had dealt very
leniently with her. At the beginning of life,
or at its end, three years are an important
period, but in the middle of existence their
weight is less perceptible. They seemed to
have passed very lightly over the small phase
of existence working itself out unheeded by
the world in the drawing-room where we
last saw Agnes Winter, and where we now
find her again.

The room was unchanged, and the Agnes
Winter dwelling therein was the same
woman except in one very small matter.
She had always been distinguished by a
cheery repose of manner which was not
without its sense of comfort for those around
her; by its presence she had acquired
the reputation of being very capable and

singularly tactful—the sort of woman, in a word, whom a clever hostess would be glad to secure at her table. This characteristic had given place to a certain restlessness— a well-concealed restlessness; but still it was there. The smile with which she now faced that grim antagonist Time was not quite so confident as of yore. Her being subtly suggested one who, having been burnt, respects the fire. Perhaps this change was more noticeable in the lady's eyes than in her person. The same strong, finished grace attended her movements, but her eyes lacked repose. They were the eyes of one who has waited and waited in vain. I need hardly say more, for we all meet the glance of such eyes frequently enough. There is a good deal of waiting to be done here below, and most of it is vain. None need search very far afield to find such eyes as now looked up nervously towards the door at the sound of the large old-fashioned bell, pealing in the basement.

"Who is that?" said Agnes Winter to herself. "Who can that be?"

She rose and set one or two things in order about the room, and after glancing at the clock, stood motionless with her tired eyes fixed on the door, listening intently. The bell was by no means a silent member of its fraternity, and there was nothing unusual in its peal, although the early hour precluded the possibility of visitors. Miss Winter had therefore no special reason for uneasiness, but people who are waiting have at times strange forebodings. While she stood there the door was opened, and the maid announced—

"Mr. Easton."

Matthew Mark Easton came into the room immediately afterwards. He shook hands rather awkwardly, as one sees a man go through the ceremony whose fingers are injured.

" How do you do, Miss Winter?" he said, gravely, managing to spread out that salutation into such length that the door was perforce closed before he had finished.

" Well," she said, in a sharp, unsteady voice, ignoring his question; "what news have you ?"

As he laid aside his hat he looked round almost furtively.

" I have no news of the ship, Miss Winter," he replied.

She begged him by a courteous gesture of the hand to take a chair, and seated herself beside the table where her work and books lay idle.

" Tell me," she said, " what you have done."

He came forward in obedience to her

wish, and in doing so emerged from the
darker side of the room into the full light
of the autumn sun. In doing this he unconsciously called attention to his own
personal appearance. The last three years
had left a twofold mark on him. In
face he was an older man, for there were a
hundred minute crow's-feet round his eyes;
and his thin cheeks, formerly sallow, now
brown and healthy, were drawn into minute
downward-tending lines; added to this was
a distinct droop at the corners of the mouth
which had always been so ready to smile.
The meaning of it all was starvation, or at
the best a lamentable insufficiency of nutri-
ment at some past period. In his form and
carriage there was a noticeable improve-
ment, for it is a remarkable thing that the
eyes and face bear far longer the marks and
results of starvation than the body that was
starved. The American was obviously a

stronger man than when Miss Winter had last seen him; his chest was broader, his step firmer, and his glance clearer.

"I have," he said, "explored every yard of the coast from the North Cape to the Yana river."

"And why did you stop at the Yana river?" asked the lady, with an air of knowing her ground.

"I will tell you afterwards," he said; "when Miss Grace is with you—if—if she does not object to my presence."

Miss Winter thought for a moment.

"No," she answered, without meeting her companion's glance; "she will like to see you, I think. I will send a note round to her at once."

She drew writing materials towards her and wrote—"Mr. Easton is here; come at once." She read it aloud, and ringing the bell, despatched the note.

"I presume," said Easton, slowly, "that the admiral is still with us."

"Yes, he is alive and well."

Easton made no comment. His manner was characterized by that singular repose which has no rest in it. He looked round him, noting little matters with a certain accuracy of observation as people do when they stand on the brink of a catastrophe. The lightness of touch which had previously characterized his social method seemed now to have left him. This was not a grave man, but a light-hearted man rendered grave by the force of circumstances. The two are quite apart. The presence of one in a room is conducive to restfulness ; the other is a disturbing element, however quiet his demeanour may be.

Miss Winter in her keener feminine sensibility was conscious of this tension, and it affected her, urging her to speak at the cost of sense or sequence.

"Helen," she said, "is . . . you will find her a little changed."

He made a convulsive little movement of his thin lips, and gasped as if swallowing something.

"Ah!" he uttered, anxiously.

"Yes; she used to take life gravely, and now . . ."

"And now, Miss Winter?"

"She is altered in that respect—you will see."

He raised his eyes to her face. His glance was as quick as ever, but his eyes did not twinkle now; they were grave, and the rapidity of their movement, being deprived of brightness, was almost furtive. He did not press the question, taking her last remark as a piece of advice, as indeed it was intended. Then they sat waiting, until the silence became oppressive. Suddenly Easton spoke with a return of the quaint narrative manner which she remembered as characteristic.

"One evening," he said, "as we were steaming down the Baltic last week—a dull warm evening, Tuesday, I guess—I was standing at the stern-rail with my arms beneath my chin when something fell upon my sleeve. I looked at it curiously, for I had not seen such a thing for years. It was a tear—most singular! I feel like crying now, Miss Winter; I should like to sit down on that low chair in the corner there and—cry. There are some disappointments that come like the disappointments of childhood—when it rained on one's birthday and put a stop to the picnic."

Miss Winter said nothing. She merely sat in her gracious, attentive attitude and looked at him with sympathetic eyes.

" It shows," he continued, presently, " how entirely one may be mistaken in one's own destiny. I never should have considered myself to be the sort of person into whose life a catastrophe was intended to break."

She still allowed him to continue, and after a pause he took advantage of her silence.

" Some men," he went on, " expect to have other lives upon their conscience— military officers, ship-captains, engine-drivers—but their own lives are more or less at equal stake, and the risk is allowed for in their salary, or is supposed to be. I have thirty lives set down on the debit side of my account, and some of those lives are chips off my own."

" Thirty ? " questioned Miss Winter. " There were only eighteen men on board, all told."

"Yes; but there were others. I shall
tell you when Miss Grace comes. It is not
a story that one cares to relate more often
than necessary."

They had not long to wait. In a few
moments they heard the sound of the
front-door bell. Easton rose from his seat.
He did not go towards the door, but stood
in the middle of the room, looking rather
breathlessly towards Miss Winter. She it
was who moved to the door and opened it,
going out to the head of the stairs to meet
Helen.

"Dear," he heard her say, and her voice
was smooth and sweet, "Mr. Easton is here;
he has come back."

There was no answer, and a moment later
Helen Grace stood before him. As he took
the hand she stretched out to him with an
air almost of bravado, he saw at once the
difference hinted at by Miss Winter. It

lay in the expression of her face, it hovered in her eyes, and yet I cannot describe it. I can only lamely set it forth on the chance of its recognition by some who have seen it in the faces around them. To those who have not encountered it, I can only say that I trust they never will, especially in their mirror. It was not recklessness, for educated women are rarely reckless, and yet it savoured of defiance—defiance of something —perhaps of the years that lay ahead. It is to be seen in most ball-rooms, and the faces carrying it are usually beautiful. The striking characteristic of such women is their impregnability. One cannot get at them. One may quarrel with them, make love to them, put them under an obligation, and never know them better. They may be sister, friend, even wife, and yet no companion. That effect of an immovable barrier never allows itself to be forgotten.

And if you meet such women, though you may be unable to define it, that barrier will make itself felt. It was placed, riveted, dovetailed, cemented by the Past—a Past in which you had no part whatever. Such a look usually goes with a perfect dress, faultless carriage, and an impeccable *savoir faire.* And Matthew Mark Easton recognized it at once, for he had lived and moved among such women, although the feminine influence in his home-life had been small.

"I am glad, Miss Grace," he said, "that you have done me the honour of coming."

And she smiled exactly as he expected—the hard inscrutable "society" smile, which never betrays, and is never infectious. She did not, however, trust herself so far as to speak. There was silence for a moment—such a silence and such a moment as leave their mark upon the entire life. Easton breathed hard. He had no doubt at that time that he was bringing to each of these women news of the man she loved.

CHAPTER XIV.

SALVAGE.

AT last he resolutely broke the silence.

"It is a long story," he said. "Will you sit down?"

Both obeyed him so mechanically and so rapidly that he had no time to prepare his words, and he hesitated.

"I—I have to tell you," he said, "that there is no news of the ship. She sailed from London three years and seven months ago. She was sighted by the whaler *Martin* on the third of May, three years ago, in the Greenland Sea, since when there is no word of her. It is the opinion of all the experts whom I have consulted that the vessel was crushed by ice, possibly a few weeks after she was sighted. Her crew and her officers have perished."

" You give us," said Miss Winter, " the opinions of others. What is your own ? "

" Mine," he said, after a pause; " mine is the same. There is no reason to suppose —there is no hope whatever."

" I gave that up two years ago," Helen stated, simply.

Easton made no comment ; but presently he drew from his pockets some thin books, which he opened, disclosing that they were maps and charts.

" I will," he said, " explain to you the theory. Here where this date is written is the spot where the ship was spoken by the whaler. She was sailing in this direction. It is probable that she passed Spitzbergen in safety, although there was ice as far

south as this thin blue line; this I have
since ascertained. After passing Spitzbergen
they would keep to the north. I take it
that at this spot they entered the broken
ice, and in all probability they were beset.
There were at the beginning of June four
separate gales of wind from the south-west.
During one or other of those gales the ship
was possibly crushed. Whether the crew
had time to take to the ice and land pro-
visions and boats, or whether it was sudden,
is a matter of conjecture. But I am quite
certain that every effort to save life, everything that was seamanlike and courageous,
was done. It failed. We have all failed.
Never was so complete an expedition fitted
up. The officers were young, but they
were good men, and for Arctic work young
men are a *sine quâ non.* What they lacked
in experience of ice-work was supplied by
their subordinate officers, who were care-

fully selected men. I can only add that
I am truly sorry I did not go with them.
I have discovered that the doctors were
wrong.   I could have stood the work, for I
have done so, and harder."

He paused, bending over the chart, which
he opened more fully, until it covered the
whole table. He seemed to be thinking
deeply, or perhaps choosing his words. The
ladies waited for him to continue.

" You see," he went on, " that all this is
conjecture; but I have something else to
tell you—something which is not a matter
of conjecture.   But first I must ask you
to—assure me—that it goes no further.   It
must be a secret sacred to ourselves, for it
is the secret of two men who—well, who
know more than we do now."

" Of course," said Miss Winter.

" Of course," echoed Helen.

He went on at once, as if anxious

to show his perfect reliance in their discretion.

" This expedition," he said, " was not despatched to discover the North-east passage. It had quite another purpose, and I have determined that in justice to my two friends you must be told. But Admiral Grace must not know. There is a political side to the question which would render his position untenable if he knew. At present the history of this generation is not yet dry—it is like a freshly-written page, and one cannot yet determine what will stand out upon it when all the writing is equally developed. But there is a huge blot, which will come out very blackly in the hereafter. When this century is history all the world will wonder why Europe was so blind to the internal condition of its greatest country. I mean Russia. It is not far from England, and yet we know more of Russia over in America than you do here. It is a long story, and we are only at the beginning of it yet; but there can only be one end. You have perhaps heard of the Nihilists, and you possibly judge them by their name. You possibly think that they are atheists, iconoclasts, miscreants. They are none of these things. They are merely a political party. They are a party of men fighting the bravest uphill fight that has been attempted. Of course there is an extreme party, the Terrorists, who, driven to despair by heartless cruelty, thirsting for revenge, or blindly impatient at the slowness of their progress, resort to violent measures. But the Nihilists must no more be judged from the Terrorist examples than your English Liberals must be confounded with Radicals."

Easton had left the table where the charts were spread. As he spoke he moved from side to side of the hearthrug, dragging his feet through the worn fur. He warmed to his work as he pleaded the cause for which he had laboured so hard, and it must be remembered that his diction was quick, almost to breathlessness,—the rapid speech of an orator, which is hardly recognizable when set down in sober black and white.

"These men," he continued, "have received singularly little help from other countries, which is accounted for by the fact that the suppression of news in Russia is an art. It is so difficult to learn the truth that most people are content with the falsehoods disseminated by the Government. But it is a singular fact that all who have studied the question, all who have lived in Russia and know anything whatever of the country, sympathize fully with the Nihilists. The contest is quite one-sided—between intellect and reckless courage on the one hand, and brutal unreasoning despotism on the other."

He paused for a moment, and then went on in a humbler tone, as if deprecating the introduction of his own personality into this great question.

" I," he said, " have given half my life to this question, and Tyars—he knew a lot about it. Together we worked out a scheme for aiding the escape of a number of the most gifted Nihilists—men and women— who had been exiled to Siberia, who were dragging out a miserable felon's existence at the mines for no other crime than the love of their own country. Our intention was not political, it was humane. We did not wish to rescue the Nihilists, but the individuals, that they might live in comparative happiness in America. Tyars and I clubbed together and supplied the funds.

I was debarred from going—forbidden by
the doctors—please never forget that. But
Tyars was the best man for the purpose
to be found anywhere, and his subordinate
officer, Oswin Grace, was even better than
Tyars in his position. A rendezvous was
fixed at the mouth of the Yana river—here
on the map—and a date was named. Three
Russians were despatched from London to
aid in the escape. They did their share.
The party arrived at the spot fixed, but the
ship—the *Argo*—never reached them. I
have been there. I have seen the dead
bodies of nine men—one of whom, Sergius
Pavloski, I knew—lying there. They seemed
to be waiting for the great Assize, when
judgment shall be given. I was quite alone,
for I expected to find something, and so
no one knows. The secret is quite safe, for
the keenest official in Siberia would never
connect the attempted escape of a number

of Nihilists with the despatch of a private
English Arctic expedition, even if the bodies
are ever found. There were no records—I
searched."

He stopped somewhat suddenly, with a
jerk, as a man stops in the narration of
something which has left an ineffaceable
pain in his life. After a little pause he
returned to the table and slowly folded the
ragged maps. The manner in which he did
so betrayed an intimate knowledge of each
frayed corner; but the movements of his
fingers were stiff and awkward. There was
a suggestion of consciousness in his every
action; his manner was almost that of a
cripple attempting to conceal his deformity.
Helen was watching him.

"And you," she inquired gently; "you
have endured great hardships?"

He folded the maps and placed them in
the breast-pocket of his coat.

" Yes," he answered, without meeting her eyes, " I have had a bad time of it."

They waited, but he said nothing more. That was the history of the last two years. Presently Helen Grace rose to go. She appeared singularly careless of detail. Part of the news she had learnt was old, the remainder was too fresh to comment upon. She kissed Miss Winter, shook hands with Matthew Mark Easton, and quickly left the room. Easton did not sit down again. He walked to the window, and standing there waited till Helen Grace had left the house, then he watched her as she crossed the road.

" These English ladies," he said, reflecting aloud, " are wonderful. They are like very fine steel."

When he turned he found Miss Winter standing beside the empty fire-place. Her attitude was scarcely an invitation for him to prolong his visit, such as might have been conveyed by the resumption of a seat.

" That," he said, buttoning his coat over the maps, " is why I did not go farther than the Yana river."

She smiled a little wearily.

" It was a wild enterprise," she said.

" I should like to try it again."

" Then it was not impossible ? "

" No," he answered, " it was not impossible."

She reflected for some moments.

" Then why did it not succeed ? "

He shrugged his shoulders.

" There is one obstacle," he answered at length, choosing his words with an unusual deliberation, " mentioned casually after others in bills of lading, policies of insurance, and other maritime documents—' the hand of God.' I surmise this was that Hand . . . and I admit that it is heavy.'

"I always felt," said Miss Winter, mus-
ingly, "that something was being concealed
from us."

"At one time I thought you knew all
about it."

Miss Winter turned and looked at him in
surprise.

"You once warned us against the Russian
minister."

She thought for some moments, recalling
the incident.

"Yes," she said at length, "I remember.
It was the merest accident. I suspected
nothing."

"Concealment," pleaded the American,
"was absolutely necessary. It made no
difference to the expedition, neither added
to the danger nor detracted from it. But
I did not want Miss Grace and yourself
to think that these two men had thrown
away their lives in attempting such a futile

achievement as the North-east passage.
They were better men than that."

She smiled a little wearily.

"No one will ever suspect," she said;
"for even now that you have told me the
story I can scarcely realize that it is true.
It sounds like some tale of bygone days;
and yet we have a living proof that it is all
true, that it has all happened."

"Helen Grace . . ." he suggested.

She nodded her head.

"Of course you knew."

"Yes," he answered, briefly.

"And did you know about him?"

He did not reply at once, but glanced
at her keenly.

"I knew that he loved her," was the
answer.

She had never resumed her seat, and he
took her attitude in the light of a dis-
missal. He made a little movement and

mechanically examined the lining of his hat.

"Are you going to stay in England?" she asked.

"No;" and he offered her his hand; "I am going back to America for some years, at all events."

They shook hands and he moved towards the door.

"When you come back to England," she said, in rather a faint voice, "will you come and see me?"

He turned sharply.

"Do you mean that, Miss Winter?"

"Yes."

His quick dancing glance was flitting over her whole person.

"If I do come," he said, with a sudden relapse into Americanism, "I surmise it will be to tell you something else—something I thought I never should tell you."

She stood quite still, a dignified, self-possessed woman, but never raised her eyes.

" Do you still mean it ? "

She gave a little nod. The door-handle rattled in his grasp, as if his hand were unsteady.

" I thought," he said, slowly, " that it was Oswin Grace."

" No."

" Never ? " he inquired, sharply.

" Never."

" Then I stay in England."

And he closed the door again.

THE END.

Richard Clay & Sons, Limited, London & Bungay.

G. C. & Co.